The Broken Circle

by G. H. Teed

First published in The Union Jack Library,
Series 2, No. 930, 30 September 1922.

Illustrated by Val Reading

Stillwoods Edition

Stillwoods.Blogspot.Ca

Catalogue Information:
Title: The Broken Circle
Author: G. H. Teed (1881-1938)
First published anonymously in The Union Jack Library, Series 2, No. 930, 30 September 1922.
Illustrated by Val Reading
This Edition by: Stillwoods, 2021, (Doug Frizzle)
ISBN Canada: 978-1-989788-58-5
Blog: Stillwoods.Blogspot.Ca
Author Blog: http://ghteed.blogspot.com/
Storefront: http://www.lulu.com/spotlight/lulubook22

Teed Bibliography Link:
https://tinyurl.com/ve25d42s
The link above should go to a spreadsheet of all known Teed stories. The list is annotated with various information on the stories and my progress with recapturing the work.   /drf

The library of Teed's stories increases almost daily. Check at the bookstore link above for the latest arrivals. /drf

Keywords: Sexton Blake, British fictional detective, Tinker, Yvonne Cartier

Cautionary Note: This series of books by Stillwoods are intended to make the stories of G. H. Teed, born in New Brunswick, Canada, available to collectors and researchers. The editor, or rather digitizer has not altered the original publication.

This story may contain language and racial terms that are not appropriate to today. I apologize for them; I know that the author was using his voice to excite and entertain an adventurous English audience. These works were published from 82 to 110 years ago. Most every work has characters of redeeming ethnicity within.

I hope you enjoy and share these stories; I have.
Doug Frizzle

This is no ordinary yarn, but a crisp and smoothly flowing narrative which will grip and hold your interest from first to last. It is the story of a broken life and a just desire for vengeance. The vivacious Yvonne on the weaker side sails very near the wind, and finds herself opposed once again to SEXTON BLAKE and TINKER— :: a yarn of quality and power. ::

Illustrated : by Val :

A STORY OF MADEMOISELLE YVONNE
COMPLETE IN THIS ISSUE.

This is no ordinary yarn, but a crisp and smoothly flowing narrative which will grip and hold your interest from first to last. It is the story of a broken life and a just desire for vengeance. The vivacious Yvonne on the weaker side sails very near the wind, and finds herself opposed once again to SEXTON BLAKE and TINKER—a yarn of quality and power.

CONTENTS of this week's Presentation DETECTIVE MAGAZINE SUPPLEMENT.

"BALMIES."

By T. C. Bridges. An extremely interesting article from the pen of this well-known writer on criminology, dealing with a very extraordinary type of prisoner.

GREAT ESCAPES.

No. 4.—JOHN WILSON.

The story of Wilson's escape from Raleigh Prison is one of the most sensational ever told. It is an account of clever foresight and dogged pluck.

POLICEWOMEN IN ROME?

By Zoe Beckley. An interesting account of the methods and work of the Italian Police.

IMITATIVE CRIMES.

By H. V. Tovey. What part does suggestion play in crime? That many crimes are imitations of others is shown in this authoritative article.

THE GHOST OF GORDON'S GAP.

Pinkerton Serial. The absorbingly interesting account of one of the most extraordinary cases ever handled by the American super-sleuth.

Fully Illustrated by Drawings & Authentic Photos.

MADEMOISELLE YVONNE laid down her private journal and glanced up as the door of her room opened to admit Miss Bryan, her confidential secretary.

"Yes, Margaret, what is it?" she said pleasantly.

"An elderly gentleman has called, mademoiselle, and insists upon seeing you. I have told him that your rule is never to see anyone who refuses to give a name, but he is very obstinate."

Yvonne mechanically reached for the big silver cigarette-box that always rested on the desk near at hand. Taking out one of the Russian cigarettes she invariably affected, she lighted it, and then gazed at her secretary thoughtfully.

"Does he appear to be a crank, Margaret? I have received several more anonymous threatening letters lately, and while I am not in the least bit nervous—" She paused to tap the handle of the drawer in which a small, but effective, automatic pistol invariably reposed, ready for instant use. "I do not wish any scenes here in the office. It might be disturbing to the other tenants of the building."

Miss Bryan blinked at her through the strong lenses of her spectacles. She had been in Yvonne's employ and confidence for a considerable time now, but daily association with her imperturbable mistress had not served to dull the admiration she felt for her.

Yvonne's cool courage and complete indifference to the threats she, like everyone else in such a profession received from time to time, were utterly beyond her understanding. Yet that did not tend to diminish the blind confidence she had in her employer. On the contrary, it but added, if anything could add, to her faith.

"Oh no mademoiselle!" answered the secretary. "He —he seems rather a nice old gentleman, very quiet and very pale, as if he had been ill for some time. He says he must consult you privately, but refuses to give his name. What shall I do?"

Yvonne shrugged faintly.

"I will break my rule for once, Margaret. Please tell him that I will see him."

The secretary murmured something and withdrew.

A few moments later the door opened again, and, as Yvonne

swiftly appraised the figure that came somewhat hesitatingly into the room, her hand, which had been hovering near the drawer in which the pistol reposed, came away and fell on the edge of the desk.

There was no danger to be apprehended from this individual.

Miss Bryan's description was correct in that the elderly man who now advanced towards Yvonne looked very pale, as if he had just recovered from a long illness.

Yvonne swiftly placed his age at somewhere around sixty-five, his status as unquestionably that of a gentleman, his character, from the thin, refined cast of countenance, as that of an ascetic, although there was a hint of strong determination of character in the jaw and his present diffident manner as a puzzling contrast which for the moment she could not understand.

He was dressed in a well-cut lounge suit of a quiet Saxony pattern; his low black shoes were undoubtedly made to order; his linen was plain white, but of excellent quality; his tie was black, giving a sombre touch, while his hat was a light grey that could only have come from one of the best hatters.

His face was quite clean-shaven, and his hair, though thin, was snowy white, well cropped and well brushed. Altogether he was extremely well groomed in an unobtrusive way.

But there was a pallor in his face and hands that was of such a dead white it puzzled Yvonne. It was not exactly that of illness, for, although his movements were hesitating, they were by no means feeble. Then suddenly a thought crossed her mind.

"This man has been in prison," she thought. "And, what is more, he has only been released very lately."

She smiled as her visitor bowed with almost old-fashioned courtesy. Then she indicated the big leather armchair that stood near her desk. Her visitor thanked her in a low, pleasant voice, and accepted the invitation.

He accepted one of Yvonne's cigarettes, and, when he had lighted it, gazed about the room as though to assure himself that there was no possibility of his being overheard.

Then his blue eyes were turned upon Yvonne in a steady scrutiny which lasted for a full minute. At last he spoke.

"So you are Mademoiselle Yvonne?" he said, almost as if he were speaking to himself "I had expected an older person."

"Perhaps I am older and wiser than I appear," responded Yvonne with another smile "My secretary informs me that you have refused to give your name, but that you wish to consult me on some matter. It is a rule of mine never to see any person who refuses his or her name, but in this instance I have broken that rule. Now, will you please give your name to me? I need not assure you that it, and whatever you may tell me, will be held in the strictest confidence.

"At the same time, you will understand that I cannot consider any case in which my client refuses these particulars. It would be working in the dark, and satisfactory results would be impossible under such conditions."

Her visitor nodded his agreement.

"I quite understand that, mademoiselle. I have no intention of suppressing my name from you. But I wanted to see what you were like before confiding in you.

"It is a very delicate matter which I have come upon, and I desired first to make sure that you were the type of person I had been led to believe you were.

"I will, with your permission, lay my case before you. I shall be perfectly frank in every way. And I shall begin by telling you who I am.

"My full name is Edward Richard Hesketh Studdington, and I am the seventh baronet of my line. Does this tell you anything? Does it recall anything to you?"

Yvonne shook her head in an effort to remember.

"It seems familiar to me," she said, "but I can't seem to remember where I have heard it before."

"You were probably too young at the time it was made notorious for it to make a lasting impression on your mind." said her visitor. "It is now about twelve years since my name was coupled with a certain great financial disaster in London. I speak of the collapse of what was known at the time as Consolidated Lands Estates of Western Canada."

"Ah!" exclaimed Yvonne. "Now I recall what you refer to. This is rather curious. My uncle —Mr. John Graves —was a shareholder in that company, and only the other day he was speaking about it.

"He was remarking that he had just received a further dividend from the trustees, and that up to now he had received back about eighty per cent of his original investment."

Sir Edward Studdington nodded.

"I am very glad to hear that. You will understand more easily what I have to tell you. It is true that since the collapse of the company shareholders have received back dividends amounting to seventy-eight per cent, to be exact, of their original investment, and by the end of next year they will have all been repaid in full.

"But this has not been due to the trustees, but was a personal liability assumed by myself and my family. I will explain.

"Consolidated Lands Estates of Western Canada was organised round a property which I held in Northern Alberta as a nucleus. This property was originally bought by my father, and for some years was run by him as a horse-ranch.

"Then at several points in that part of the country oil was found, some of the wells being of commercial value and some petering out soon after the first outflow. My father died about that time, and I, who had had little experience of business, continued to run the place as a horse-ranch.

"Myself, I was completely engrossed in my hobby —Egyptology —which, as you will realise, does not make a very desirable bedfellow for company promotion.

"It was about this time that wells were sunk at several places close to my own property, and, as some of them appeared to be of some value, I yielded to the persuasions of a certain group of financiers in the City and permitted them to prospect on my estate.

"Wells were sunk at several points, and following that, a large company was formed by London and New York financiers, with, as I have said, my estate as the nucleus.

"Well, I was made president of the consolidated companies, and the shares were offered for public subscription, accompanied by glowing reports of the golden future offered by the investment.

If you will look up the financial reports covering that time you will find that there was a tremendous boom in oil shares, and our issue was oversubscribed several times. Moreover, there was a terrific lot of wild speculation in the shares, and then, when I was still dazed from my sudden plunge into a strange world, the crash came.

"I shall not dilate on what followed. I can scarcely realise it all even now, after twelve years in which to think of it. It seems that the wells were mere pocket gushers, and most of them soon petered out, while those that continued to run did not yield enough to warrant any dividend on the shares.

"Investigations revealed that not only had there been criminal

4

misrepresentation in the promotion of the company, but that there had been fraudulent practices as well. And in every case this had been done under my signature.

"I said then, and I say now, that I signed everything that was put before me, and not until the crash came did I realise that it was my name as president, and my name only, that must stand the responsibility. I do not excuse myself. It was criminal ignorance, if you will.

"I ought never to have allowed myself to be made the tool of those sharks, who fattened on the company and then before the crash came got out, each with a fortune.

"I turned over every penny of my own money for the benefit of the shareholders. But that was only a drop in the bucket. There were so many charges, and so many small shareholders had lost their all, that I was given the maximum sentence on my conviction —fifteen years."

The old man paused, and drew a shaky hand across his face as if to wipe away some ugly vision. Then he proceeded:

"My friends all fell away from me. They could not believe —and I do not blame them —that a man could be such a fool as to sign the documents I signed without knowing something of their purport.

"But I assure you, on my life, mademoiselle, that those papers were to me an unwritten language. An inscription on an Egyptian temple would have been perfectly clear. But I accepted the assurances of those into whose hands I had fallen that they were quite in order.

"It was I who paid the penalty for my own criminal ignorance — for it was criminal ignorance for me to accept a position of such trust and responsibility without the requisite knowledge to govern my acts wisely. However, that is past.

"At the time of the settlement of the company's affairs all the various properties were thrown on the market, and, mademoiselle, the very men who had looted the public through that promotion —the men who had covered up their acts under my ignorance —bought most of them in at bargain prices, if I may use the term.

"Not all of them, for some, they knew, were quite worthless. But those which they knew quite well could be made commercially profitable they bought, and operated them on private account.

"During the period of time which elapsed before my trial I set myself to try to grasp some of the elemental of the whole problem.

"I came to the conclusion that I was in honour bound, no matter whether I was sentenced to a term of imprisonment or not, to reimburse to the shareholders every penny they had invested in the companies.

"As I have said, my own personal fortune was but a drop in the bucket, but my daughter had some money of her own which came to her through her grandmother. We had a conference —my son, my daughter, and I —and we determined to buy back the property that had originally been mine. We did this, and when I entered prison my son took over the development of the estate.

"He drove several fresh wells, and in a very short time struck rich shale deposits. Two gushers proved to be permanent wells, and, in fact, they still average between them almost a thousand barrels of oil per day. It is from the sale of that oil that the shareholders have been repaid a certain amount year by year. It is from the money thus received that your uncle has received his dividends. And, as I have stated payments will be continued until every claim has been wiped out.

"It has been necessary for me to deal with these facts in some detail in order that you may grasp the situation clearly. Now for the reasons that brought me to you. Shortly after I begun to serve my sentence my dear wife died —died of the shock and disgrace. Then the war broke out, and my son immediately rejoined his regiment while my daughter took up nursing. My son was killed in France in the early days of the war, and at the present time my daughter is confined in a sanatorium.

"Her health is completely broken.

"You may understand that when these tidings reached me in prison I became embittered with —well, with everything. My one aim in life grew to be to exact vengeance on those who had brought all this sorrow and misery and disgrace upon me. Then it chanced that I was placed in charge of the prison library, and during the time I spent there I had access to journals and books which I might otherwise never have seen.

"That was when I first heard of you, mademoiselle. I came upon an article in a magazine dealing with certain events in your life, and I went back through other issues of that journal until I had read all I could about you.

"After that I began to think.

"I said to myself: 'If this young girl, left alone in Australia as she was, orphaned and ruined by a group of soulless capitalists, could devote her life to a just vengeance which the law denied her. Then is it impossible for me, a man —albeit an old man and a broken one — to do likewise?' You, a girl, found your vengeance within the law. You, a girl, made those men, each and every one of them, pay the penalty. And I swore that what you did then I could do.

"From that day the idea grew upon me until it obsessed me. It was my every thought, sleeping or waking. I lived but for the day of my release, when I could begin my vengeance,

"And then it slowly came to me that I would come to you, tell you all, seek your advice, and ask you to help me. As you know, there is a certain remission of sentence due to what the prison authorities call 'good behaviour.'

"As my prison record was clean. I received the full benefit of this, and instead of serving the full term of fifteen years I was released after about twelve years.

"I came out of prison a week age. I have interviewed the trustees whom my son appointed to run the Canadian estate when he went to France, and I find that everything is going very satisfactorily. They assure me that at the end of this year it will be possible to pay off the balance of twenty-two per cent still due to investors. Then the slate will be clear so far as I am concerned.

"But I shall not rest until I have brought to book those creatures who have brought this ruin and shame upon my life. I want vengeance, and I will have it! I have sufficient funds to pay the necessary expenses. That is my story, mademoiselle. I have come to you. Will you help me?"

As he finished speaking the old man leant back, almost exhausted. The raking up of all the old tortures, the scarifying of the old wounds had taken all his strength.

Yvonne rose from her seat, and, crossing quickly to a cabinet which stood in one corner, took out a small flagon of brandy. She poured a generous measure, into which she splashed a little soda. Then she returned to her visitor.

When he had gulped down the strong spirit a little colour came into his cheeks, and he thanked her gratefully. Yvonne set the glass down and reseated herself. She did not speak until she had lighted a fresh cigarette. Then she said:

"Because I have not interrupted your story, Sir Edward, does not mean that I have not been interested, or that I have not understood. I have, most vividly, for it has taken me back to the days in Australia when I was only a young girl, full of misery and pain, and seeking blindly to hurt those who had brought ruin upon my dear, trusting father and my helpless little mother.

"I can sympathise very deeply with you, and I can understand your desire to exact vengeance. In that I am in accord with you, providing you do not seek such vengeance by flouting the written law of the land.

"In my own impetuosity I ran dangerously close at times to the border, so close, indeed, that on one occasion I had to go through the experience that you yourself have just been through. That taught me a lesson, for it might have prevented me from bringing to book those who were still untouched

"The men who ruined you, like those who ruined us, could not be reached by what we term our courts. They had been too clever but morally they had broken every law of honour and right.

"If it is your purpose to bring them down into the dust —to fight for their ruin one after the other —then you may count on me to assist you with every weapon in my power. That is the main aim of my life —to bring to book those whom the law does not reach, and, in helping you, I shall find it a work after my own heart.

"If, on those conditions, you still wish my aid, then it is yours, and we can get down to a discussion just as soon as you wish."

"Heaven bless you, mademoiselle, for those words. I do wish your aid —on any terms you may name."

"In that case, there is no time like the present for a beginning." responded Yvonne with a smile. "I will inform my secretary that I am not to be disturbed, and we can get to work. By the way, Sir Edward, how many of these men are there?"

"Eight in all."

"That is rather a curious coincidence —it is the same number that, I, myself, had to deal with. Uncle will certainly be interested in this. Will you lunch with us? He will be so glad to meet you."

"Why, that is most kind of you, mademoiselle! I —I should be delighted! I am afraid I am at rather a loose end," he added wistfully.

"We shall soon make up for that," rejoined Yvonne cheerfully as she rang for Miss Bryan.

When she had given instructions that she was not to be disturbed the old man drew up his chair, and together they began to go into the details of the case. And as she jotted down notes from time to time, a curious zest began to take hold of Yvonne. She felt, somehow, that she was on the brink of new things —which she was, with a vengeance.

II. *A Whitewashed Britisher —And a Speech In Vienna —Yvonne Does Some Arithmetic —Setting a Trap.*

SOME three weeks after the first visit of Sir Edward Studdington, Mademoiselle Yvonne sat at the desk in her private room engrossed upon a study of a mass of notes which had been collected during that period of time. While it had been three weeks of rather tiring and boresome seeking after facts and data, the result had been far from unsatisfactory from Yvonne's point of view.

Following the details which her latest client had given her, Yvonne had ticked off the first name on the list, and had set herself to discover all she could about the man whom she intended should be the first to receive her attention.

From Sir Edward she had been able to discover little beyond the name —Otto Bernstorm —and that he was "some sort of a financier in the City." But through her own sources of information, together with the English and Continental newspaper clipping agencies to which she subscribed, it did not take Yvonne very long to discover a good deal about the said Otto Bernstorm.

She discovered that he was an Austrian by birth, that he had come to London as a very young man, and had soon become identified with certain company promoting circles in the City.

Later on he had become naturalised, and, during the war, had publicly reiterated his unswerving loyalty (sic) to the British Empire. This loyalty had not prevented him from taking advantage of the abnormal conditions following upon the war in order to pile up a very considerable fortune, although, from what Yvonne was able to discover, he had dropped a great portion of that after the armistice, when the general slump had it struck the country.

At the time Yvonne began to take an interest in him, he was a little over fifty years of age, was still engaged in the City, still kept up his mansion in Upper Brook Street, and was, to all intents and purposes, as prosperous as ever.

But Yvonne's secret information revealed that there was far less behind this outward show than was generally thought. And she had patiently probed away until she had discovered a good deal about Mr. Otto Bernstorm's more recent activities than his closest friends suspected.

She found that, like a good many other financiers, Otto

Bernstorm had taken a "view" of foreign exchange some time before, and that, like many more, he had been badly "bitten."

But, unlike these others, his facile brain had taken a still longer view, and, following a visit to Vienna, where, it appeared, he still had considerable interests, he, in company with certain other financiers, had embarked upon a measured campaign by which they proposed making up their losses by manipulating exchange as they wished it to go.

In that circumstance, Yvonne came upon the first thing that seemed to offer a chance of finding the weak spot which she sought in Otto Bernstorm's activities. Therefore, she had concentrated all her efforts to discover just what he had been up to in the exchange speculation line, and a study of the figures which now lay before her would have been highly interesting and diverting to several persons in the City, not least among whom would have been Otto Bernstorm's colleagues.

For, true to his nature, Bernstorm had been unable to resist the temptation to "double cross" those colleagues when he found it to his own profit to do so.

Instead of pooling his own gains with the general fund, Bernstorm had gradually turned the money into good sterling bearer-bonds; and, more than that, had been gradually getting rid of his investments in Austria to convert the proceeds into English money.

When this speculation on the part of Bernstorm and his friends had started the Austrian crown had stood at something like seven thousand to the pound sterling, as against a normal pre-war exchange of only twenty-four to the pound. On this day on which Yvonne was studying the numerous facts she had collected, the Austrian exchange was no less than one hundred and thirty thousand crowns to the pound sterling, or, in other words, almost worthless.

Therefore, she found a peculiar interest in the translation she had made from a clipping culled from a Vienna newspaper which her Continental agency had sent her. It referred to a speech made by Otto Bernstorm during a recent visit to Vienna.

At that time the crown been quoted at about twenty thousand to the pound, and, in answer to nervous inquiries made of him at a dinner in Vienna, Bernstorm was quoted as saying:

"It is all nonsense to talk of the crown decreasing in value any further. We are passing through a difficult time, but to prove to you my own confidence in the crown, I will tell you that instead of selling it for foreign currency, I am buying it and putting it away for a recovery in value. And I will say this, that no matter what fluctuations there may be in the exchange, I am prepared to accept now and at any future time crowns for any sterling or dollar investments I hold at not more than twenty-five thousand to the pound. That is how I feel about this question."

Brave words all right, but every syllable a lie, as Yvonne's information told her. Otto Bernstorm had not been buying Austrian crowns when he made that boast, but had been secretly selling them as fast as he could. Not only had he been liquidating sterling and dollar investments and putting the money into crowns, to hold for a rise in value, but he had been quietly getting rid of his Austrian investments through a dummy name, and turning the proceeds into sterling bearer bonds.

Yvonne had indisputable proof of this. And she knew, furthermore, that, on the very day he had made that speech, when crowns had naturally risen a little in value, he had at once made further purchases of sterling.

Oh, it was a shrewd and cunning game that Otto Bernstorm had been playing, and his cunning was never more exemplified than in the way he had been able to hoodwink not only his dupes in Vienna, but his colleagues in London as well.

But in one sentence in that speech of his Yvonne thought she had found what she needed. That sentence which said, "And I will say this, that no matter what fluctuations there may be in the exchange, I am prepared to accept now and at any future time, crowns for any sterling or dollar investments I hold at not more than twenty-five thousand to the pound."

Easy words to utter, and easy enough to repudiate should the statement recur to anyone, and they, in their ignorance, should try to hold him to them with crowns at one hundred and thirty thousand to the pound!

It was, however, on the basis of this statement which had issued from his own lips that Yvonne proposed to deal. She proposed taking him at his own value, and in this way try to carry out the first step in her new campaign of vengeance. How was she to do it?

She tapped her teeth with the tip of her pencil, and frowned at the maze of figures.

Beside the papers she had been studying was a small notebook containing the eight names which Sir Edward Studdington had given her. Opposite each name was the amount which each man must be held responsible for. The total amounts which Sir Edward Studdington would have to meet before all the investors in Consolidated Lands Estates were paid off in full amounted to one hundred and thirty nine thousand pounds sterling.

Yvonne had thought the simplest plan would be to divide this amount equally among the eight financiers who had precipitated the ruin, and as the division did not go quite exactly, she placed the amount in round figures at fifteen thousand pounds sterling each, which seemed fair enough.

"Fifteen thousand pounds from Otto Bernstorm, to begin with," she murmured. "From the information I have received there must be several times that amount in bearer-bonds in Bernstorm's private safe in the library of his house in Upper Brook Street. And nothing else but bearer-bonds would be safe for us to take. Now, let me see just how I can arrange this.

"To begin with, Mr. Bernstorm committed himself to the statement in Vienna that he would always be prepared to exchange either sterling or dollar investments for Austrian crowns at not more than twenty five thousand crowns to the pound. I wonder how he feels about that with exchange where it is to-day?

"However, we shall have a chance to find out before long. And the beauty of it is, he won't dare make a public protest for fear of his own secret activities coming out. But he will not take it without striking back — of that I am certain.

"Well, we shall be prepared for him, and if he isn't good, then we shall be compelled to penalise him still further.

"Now for the exact figures. Fifteen thousand pounds, Mr. Bernstorm's share of the penalty, would amount in Austrian crowns at twenty-five thousand crowns to the pound to the sum of no less than three hundred and seventy-five million crowns.

"On the other hand, to buy three hundred and seventy-five million crowns at to-day's exchange it would only cost about three thousand pounds, or a little less. All right, Mr. Bernstorm, I will just add the round sum of three thousand pounds to your fifteen thousand-pounds' penalty, for, of course, you must provide our working capital and expenses as well. That makes eighteen thousand pounds in all, or, at your exchange of twenty-five thousand crowns to the pound, a total of four hundred and fifty million crowns.

"Just for good measure, I will add another fifty million crowns for expenses, which sounds a lot, but isn't really very much.

"That is exactly five hundred million crowns. There, Mr. Bernstorm, we shall test your words with that sum to start with, and, if you are not good, perhaps we shall give them a further test. And now I wonder if I can find so many crowns in London?"

With that, Yvonne lifted the telephone-receiver, and got through to her broker in the City.

That individual gasped at her cool request that he buy at once Austrian currency to the extent of five hundred million crowns. He warned her that it might prove a risky investment, as the exchange might go still lower. But Yvonne laughed at his protests, and instructed him to collect the necessary amount as quickly as possible.

That done, she glanced at her watch, to find that it was a few minutes after three o'clock. As she expected a visitor at three, she rang her bell to advise Miss Bryan that she was now at liberty, and a few seconds later the door of her private room opened, to admit a young woman, who bore the stamp of the respectable upper-class servant. Yvonne smiled at her, and motioned her into the big armchair by the desk.

"Well, Stella, I see you were able to get away," she remarked, as she leant back and lighted a cigarette. "How is your brother getting on now?"

"Very well indeed, miss," answered the girl. "I was at home last night, and told him I was coming to see you to-day. He told me to tell you that he is to be made head shipping-clerk on the first of next month. It's all thanks to you that he is, miss!"

The girl referred to a case in which Yvonne had been able to prove that her brother, employed in the shipping department of a big London firm, and accused of pilfering, had been innocent.

The lad's sister, having heard of Yvonne, had come to her in tears, and Yvonne had at once taken up the case. She had soon discovered that the pilfering was the work of another shipping-clerk and a driver, who had worked things so that the blame should fall on young Bentley, the brother of the girl who now sat in Yvonne's office.

Needless to say their gratitude —for Yvonne had refused to take any fee —had been deep, and when Yvonne had sent word to the girl to come and see her the first afternoon she was able to get out, the other lost no time in doing so.

Yvonne's request was based on the fact that Stella Bentley happened to be second housemaid in Otto Bernstorm's house in Upper Brook Street. It was an instance where circumstances favoured her plans, but if such had not been the case, then she would simply have found another way to her goal.

"I am very pleased, indeed, to hear that, Stella. And how are you getting on in your own place?"

"Very well, miss, thank you! Only I shall probably be leaving in a month or two."

"Why is that?" asked Yvonne quickly. "Are you dissatisfied?"

"Oh, no, miss! But, you see, I —I —" And she coloured.

Yvonne laughed.

"Oh! It is that is it, Stella —you are going to be married?"

"Yes, miss."

"That is splendid! I hope you have chosen well. You must let me know when it is to be. And now, Stella, I have asked you to come here for a very particular reason. But before I tell you what it is I want to put your mind at rest.

"What I am going to ask you is something you need not have the slightest fear of doing. You know that I would not touch anything of a dishonourable nature, and, while there are things about the request I am going to make that may puzzle you, you need not be at all uneasy.

"Even if I told you all you would not understand, for the details are very complicated, dealing with money and exchange and several other things. Do you believe me?"

The girl's eyes glowed with a perfect trust.

"Of course, I believe you, miss! Why, I just know you couldn't do anything wrong! And if I can help you in anything, I shall be only too glad of the chance. I can never do enough to repay you for what you have I done for me and mine!"

"Thank you, Stella," said Yvonne quietly. "That was nice of you, and I know you meant it. Now, listen, and I will tell you what I want you to do for me."

Forthwith, Yvonne began to speak in low, earnest tones, and, as she proceeded, the listening girl nodded her head from time to time. At last, when Yvonne had finished, other said:

"Why, of course. I will do all that, miss —just as you have said. It will be fun, and I don't mind the risk a bit. Jim —I mean, my young man, would understand if I told him; and, anyway, he says Mr. Bernstorm is only a whitewashed Britisher, who did nothing during the war but make patriotic speeches and pile up money."

"Your young man is a person of discernment," remarked Yvonne with a smile. "I certainly must meet him one day. And now, Stella, I am going to give you a cup of tea. Then, when you go back, be ready to do what I have explained when you hear from me."

"I will that, miss. You can depend on me."

Yvonne nodded and rang for the redheaded office-boy, whose proud duty it was each day to bring Yvonne her tea.

And thus it was that Yvonne set her trap —a trap that was sprung exactly three days later, when her amazed broker had turned over to her the colossal (on paper) sum of five hundred million Austrian crowns.

End of the Prologue.

The First Chapter.   Exchange no Robbery —Blake Gets to Work — The Blushing Maidservant —What Bernstorm Kept Back —The Sign of the Derrick.

"THOSE are the bare facts, Mr. Blake. I can tell you no more than that. The whole thing is a blank mystery as far as I am concerned. That is why I have called you in."

Otto Bernstorm was sitting at the big mahogany desk in the library of his house in Upper Brook Street. Opposite him was Sexton Blake, the famous criminologist, who had come to Upper Brook Street that morning at the urgent behest of Bernstorm.

In one corner of the room was a large, very modern safe, which had been the subject of Otto Bernstorm's remarks, for, as he finished speaking, he waved his hand towards it.

"I quite understand that, Mr. Bernstorm," rejoined Sexton Blake dryly, even though he was, at the moment, smoking one of the other's cigars. "But you must understand that in any case every little point, no matter how trivial it may appear, has a certain value in the construction of the general fabric. Now let us just run over the facts again.

"You say that in this safe here you had a hundred and ten thousand pounds worth of bearer bonds. You are certain that they were intact last evening, owing to the fact that shortly after dinner it was necessary for you to go to the safe, and you took occasion then to go through the daily checking."

"Quite right."

"Then this morning you again went to the safe, and at once noticed that something was wrong. On investigating, you discovered that a quantity of the bonds had been taken —twenty thousand pounds, to be exact. And to your amazement, in place of these missing bonds you found Austrian paper currency to the amount of five hundred million crowns."

"That is so"

"Very well. At present exchange, five hundred million crowns only amount to about four thousand pounds, or, as a matter of fact, under that. Therefore, if you converted these crowns today into sterling —and I do not think you would find it easy to do so —then your net loss would amount to about sixteen thousand pounds, or, say, a little more."

"Exactly."

"And yet you found the safe combination apparently in perfect order? I haven't had a chance yet to examine it, but I shall do so presently. For the moment I accept your statement.

"Now, think well, please. Is there any little thing you have forgotten? Is there anything relating to your business in the City that would help us?

"Have you any reason to suppose that any one there might have sufficient motive to abstract twenty thousand pounds in bonds from your safe and substitute Austrian crowns in their stead? Incidentally, Mr. Bernstorm, isn't it rather an odd amount to place there?

"And why should the thieves leave anything at all? Let me see, if we apply that amount of crowns to the amount of bonds missing, it would work out at —hm! —why, exactly twenty-five thousand crowns to the pound. That can have no relation to the exchange value, for I see by the morning papers that crowns are quoted at one hundred and twenty-eight thousand to the pound, as against one hundred and thirty thousand a couple of days or so ago."

"The amount has no relation to the exchange value," rejoined Otto Bernstorm rather irritably. "I don't know what fool idea is behind the leaving of this Austrian currency in the safe. It can't have anything to do with a forced exchange upon me. I tell you I have no idea.

"As I have already explained to you, Mr. Blake. I have sent for you because this is a matter on which I do not care to consult Scotland Yard.

"I am at present engaged in some important transactions in the City, and it is essential that the affair should be kept quiet. That is why I called you in. I know that you can go to work and run the thing down without any publicity. Just find out who did it. That is all I ask.

"And when you have found them, don't make any arrests. I only want to know who is behind it. Then I will deal with them."

"You set me rather a difficult problem, Mr. Bernstorm. You ask me to run the thieves to earth, and yet you would tie my hands. I never, under any circumstances, work under those conditions. I must have a free hand."

"All right. Use your own methods, but find them!" snapped the financier savagely. "This means a lot to me, outside of the actual money loss. In view of the transactions I am engaged upon, it is essential that I know who is behind it. I don't for a moment believe that it was done by ordinary thieves. I feel certain that it was pulled off by someone who knows a good deal about my business. There are certain things that make me think that."

"As, for instance?"

"The presence of that Austrian currency, for one thing."

"Yes, I am inclined to agree with you there. Have you any reason to suspect anyone in your employ —either in the City or here in your own house?"

"No. The only person in my office who knows anything about my private transactions is my secretary, and I can vouch for him." (Otto Bernstorm had good reason to feel so sure on this point, considering that if he chose, he could have sent his secretary to prison for an old misdemeanour.)

"And, as far as the house is concerned, no one here could open that safe. No, Mr. Blake, it was done by outsiders, but how they managed to get into the house, open that safe, and get out again, I can't imagine. It was done between ten o'clock last night and seven o'clock this morning —that much is beyond dispute."

"You have questioned your servants?"

"Naturally. I retired myself about half-past eleven. The butler locked up himself after I went upstairs. None of the servants were out, and everyone was in bed by midnight. This morning none of the windows or doors were found unlatched or disturbed, and yet those bonds were gone."

Blake nodded.

"It is certainly mysterious. However, my assistant will be here any moment now. He is rather sharp on such things, and I will have him make another examination of the windows and doors. In the meantime, I shall have a look at this room and the safe. Afterwards, just as a matter of form, I should like to have a word with each of the servants."

"All right. I will tell the butler to have them in readiness."

Laying down the end of his cigar, Blake rose, and taking out his pocket glass, strolled across to the safe. As he bent over it he murmured:

"Good safe —right up to date, and one of the latest combinations. H'm! Not impossible to an expert hand, and particularly if one was equipped with a microphone; but even at that it would take some time.

If it was done last night after they all went to bed, then it was done by a mighty cool and a mighty capable hand. Now, let us see what we can see."

He began his examination at the combination, but turned his head presently with the curt request that the curtains be pulled aside from the window in order that he might have more light.

Then he proceeded, studying every particle of the shiny nickel knob and disc. "Little use to test for finger-prints," he thought as he worked. "Whoever did this job would certainly have used gloves, and besides, in opening it this morning Bernstorm would have wiped off any prints. I don't love you, Mr. Bernstorm, but you have provided me with a mighty interesting case, or I am greatly mistaken. Hallo! What is this—"

Blake had come upon something that held his keen attention, for now his thoughts broke off, and he concentrated every faculty on the matter in hand. It wasn't much that he saw —just the tiniest of marks; but if he could locate its fellow, where it might be, then he knew that he had made one discovery.

And just where it ought to have been was the second mark —very faint; but still it was there, and, as he passed on to another part, Sexton Blake knew that he had confirmed one thing, at any rate —a microphone had been used, as he had suspected.

He was interrupted at that point by the appearance of Tinker. He broke off long enough to give Tinker instructions to examine all the basement and ground-floor doors and windows, then he returned to the safe; but although he persisted for another half hour he found nothing else of any value.

Nor did Tinker have anything to report. He had gone over every possible means of entrance on both the ground floor and the basement floor, and Blake was quite satisfied that if Tinker had found nothing, then there was nothing to be found.

The examination of the servants —nine in all —proved as abortive as Otto Bernstorm had prophesied, although, as he studied the facial expressions of each while he questioned them, Blake wondered a little at the quick flushing and paling of one of the housemaids.

He was rather inclined, however, to dismiss it as sheer nervousness on her part, for she was a bright-looking girl with a pleasant, frank expression, and not at all the sort one would associate with collusion in such a theft as had taken place the night before.

At the same time, in view of the results of Tinker's examination, it certainly looked as if there had been assistance from someone inside the house. While Blake did not entirely dismiss that possibility from his mind, he shelved it for the moment, determining to probe the possibility more deeply should things seem to warrant.

Then he and Tinker took their departure, after Blake had informed Otto Bernstorm that he would communicate with him as soon as he had anything to report.

Things might have been less difficult for Blake had Otto Bernstorm been perfectly frank with him. But the financier had not told all, despite his assurances to the contrary. He had not informed Blake that, just under the rubber band which had been slipped round the bundle of Austrian notes, he had found a clipping from an Austrian newspaper, as well as a piece of plain white paper on which had been rather crudely sketched a tall derrick, such as one sees above an oil well.

" I cannot see him," snapped Otto Bernstorm. " You should know bet'er than
to disturb me ! "   But at that moment the clerk was swept aside by the thrust
of a powerful hand, and the stranger entered.   (*Chapter 2.*)

The Second Chapter. *A Faithful Servant —And a Disturbing Discovery —An Angry Compatriot —A Promise Recalled —Stern Measures.*

As soon as Sexton Blake and Tinker had departed, Otto Bernstorm entered his waiting motor, and drove through to his offices in Crosby Square, just off Bishopsgate Street. When he had laid aside his coat and hat he seated himself at his desk and rang at once for Franklin, his confidential clerk. Directly the door had closed after the clerk, Bernstorm motioned for him to come close to the desk.

"Franklin, you remember the case some years ago of the Consolidated Lands Estates, when Studdington was sentenced to fifteen years imprisonment?"

"Yes, sir —it was ten or twelve years ago."

"Twelve years. Studdington got fifteen years, you remember. Now, it had not occurred to me that there is usually a remission of sentence for what is known as 'good behaviour.'

"I have been figuring things out, and if Studdington received any such benefit his term ought to be about up. I want you to make immediate inquiries, and find out if he has been released, or is about to be released. Do this before anything else, and let me know just as soon as you can. It is important."

"Very good, sir."

Franklin, the man over whom Otto Bernstorm held the whip of exposure should he fail to do his bidding in any way he might demand, departed upon his errand.

Not only did he remember the case to which his master had referred, but he also knew that Sir Edward Studdington had been the scapegoat for frauds that Bernstorm and his associates at the time had been guilty of.

Had he possessed more spirit he might have used his knowledge to free himself from the noose which Bernstorm continually dangled before him, for, after all, his own misdemeanour had not been a very serious one. But the fear of exposure, the dread of leaving an old and crippled mother without protection or support, had gradually sapped whatever manhood he had once possessed, until he had become nothing but a colourless echo of Bernstorm's wishes.

Therefore, while he felt a vague stirring of curiosity as to why his employer was apparently so anxious to discover news of the man he had had a hand in ruining so many years ago, it never occurred to him to try and turn the fact to his own advantage. Instead, he meekly did as he was bid.

He figured the best line of inquiry to take would be to get in touch with a certain private inquiry agent whom Bernstorm had employed on different occasions. And in less than an hour his decision was justified, for the agent informed him that Sir Edward Studdington had been released from prison a little over a week.

With that information Franklin returned to his master, whom he found bent over his desk, apparently deeply engrossed in a slip of paper. Just before he thrust it away the clerk noticed that it seemed to have some sort of sketch drawn on it, but what it was he could not make out.

"Well," snapped Bernstorm shortly.

"I have made the inquiry, sir. Studdington was released from prison a little over a week ago."

"My heavens! Then it must be so! There can be no one else. But how has he dared? He never showed such initiative in the old days. It seems incredible, and yet who else could it be? Who else would leave that sketch. It can only refer to one thing."

"I don't wish to be impertinent, sir, but may I ask —"

Bernstorm struck the desk irritably.

"Listen, Franklin! As you know, I have been quietly doing a good deal in Austrian exchange privately, in addition to the pool in which I am interested. The sterling funds I have received from these private transactions I have been investing in bearer script, which I kept in the safe at my house.

"Last night someone entered my house and got into the safe. They took away twenty thousand pounds' worth of bearer-bonds, and left in their place five hundred million crowns in Austrian currency — worth at today's exchange under four thousand pounds.

"At first I thought it might have been done by some member of the pool with which I am working —someone who had discovered that I was also operating privately.

"You know, of course, that no member is supposed to carry on any exchange transactions outside of the pool. But then I found on top of the bundle of notes a newspaper clipping and a sketch. The clipping was from an Austrian paper, and was part of a report of a fool speech I made some weeks ago in Vienna, after a dinner there.

The sketch was of an oil well derrick. That made me think.

"I sent for Sexton Blake, the criminologist, to investigate matters —for, of course, I can't call in the police. He now has the matter in hand, but I told him nothing about the clipping or the sketch.

"I wanted first to think it over. Well, the sketch made me think of Studdington, and now that you tell me he has been out of prison for more than a week, it looks as if he must have had a hand in this business. But I'll wager he never pulled it off by himself, he has had someone to help him. And what we must do is to locate him without delay. I must find him, and soon. Do you understand?

"It is possible that he has got in touch with some member of the exchange pool, and they have pulled this on me. I can't tell yet, but I want you to turn Reinhardt, the inquiry agent, on to that at once.

"I don't want to tell Sexton Blake about it. As a matter of fact, I am sorry now that I called him in. I should have left it to Reinhardt. I will choke Blake off as soon as possible. But in the meantime, you see Reinhardt, and start him off after Studdington at once. At once! Do you understand?"

"Yes, sir. I think, sir, I had better go and see Reinhardt. It would not be quite wise to telephone."

"Quite so. My car is outside. Go in that, and impress Reinhardt with what I say. He must get after Studdington at once. Tell him to put everything else on one side."

"Very good, sir. I shall report immediately on my return."

With that, the colourless but faithful Franklin took his departure.

Now, spineless as he might be where his master was concerned, the financier's confidential clerk was obstinate enough in carrying out his master's instructions, and it was for this reason that undesirable visitors found it more difficult to get past him than would have been the case with a clerk who held Bernstorm in less fear.

And it is safe to say that, had Franklin not been away from the office, that which followed shortly after his departure to see Reinhardt would not have occurred.

He had been gone about a quarter of an hour, and Otto Bernstorm was still engrossed with the curious sketch that had been slipped under the rubber band which had held the mysterious notes together, when there came a knock at the door of his private room.

In answer to his gruff command the door opened, to admit one of the junior clerks from the main office.

"Please sir," he said hesitatingly, "there is a gentleman who insists upon seeing you. I have asked him if he has an appointment, but he says he has not."

"Did he give his name?"

"No, sir. He refused to do so, but insists on seeing you. He says he will not go away until he has done so."

"I cannot see him!" snapped Otto Bernstorm. "You should know better than to disturb me! You know the rules of the office. Send him away. If he refuses to go, then call the police and have him removed!"

"Very good, sir; I will do so!"

But the clerk was not to have an opportunity of carrying out his instructions, for at that moment the door was jerked open, and he was swept aside by a powerful hand. As he staggered away a man entered the room —a man who glowered upon the financier, then snapped out something in Magyar.

Otto Bernstorm sat rigid for a few seconds, his face revealing nothing of what was in his mind. Bernstorm's "poker face" had been of great value to him on more than one occasion in the past, and, while he knew only too well why this stranger had forced his way into his private office, he did not betray the slightest agitation before his clerk. Instead, he said, curtly:

"You may go, Clifford, I will see this gentleman —now that he is here."

The clerk retired, but not until the door had closed after him did the stranger speak. He was a big, swarthy individual of distinct Magyar type, and, although his clothes were neat enough, they showed signs of long wear.

It was plain that he was labouring under some strong emotion, for his face showed signs of the ravages of sleeplessness, and his eyes were filled with a light that an experienced observer would have known meant danger.

But Otto Bernstorm, to give him credit, faced the other coolly. Like his visitor, he spoke in Magyar.

"Well," he said quietly, "it is a surprise to see you in London, my friend! What has brought you here?"

"You know very well what has brought me here," answered the other, with an effort to remain calm. "You received my letters?"

"I had two —yes."

"Why didn't you answer them?"

"What was there for me to say? You can read. You have seen the papers. You know to what level exchange has dropped. What more is there I could add?"

"A great deal. Since you would not reply to my letters, I have taken from the last of the funds I possess to come to London to see you. You do not deny that I, like many others in Vienna, have lost my all because I believed what you told us?"

Bernstorm shrugged.

"I do not know what you mean," he said. "If you mean that because, when I was in Vienna, I spoke optimistically, then you cannot blame me. What would you have me say? Would you have had me condemn Austrian conditions and Austrian currency?

"You ought to know that when a financier is visiting a country, and is asked to say something for publication, he invariably speaks in an optimistic vein. It is only polite to one's hosts."

"I do not deny that. But you were not a mere visitor to Austria. You were born there, and your visit was for the sole purpose of speculating in the exchange of the country. Moreover, it was on your advice that I and others tried to retrieve what we had lost by the terrible slump in values there.

"In Vienna you made a categorical statement, and, on behalf of my friends and myself, I wrote to you to hold you to that statement. You did not even answer my letters, so I have come to ask you here and now if you propose standing by that statement. I know a good deal about your activities, Bernstorm, and I know that you have not played straight.

"You may be able to get away with that in London, but through you I and many others are ruined, and we demand satisfaction! If you had been honest, then we would have taken our losses, and said nothing. But you tricked us; the money we lost has gone into your pockets!"

"You must be mad. I haven't the faintest idea what you mean?"

"You lie! Did you not say in Vienna, during the course of a speech there, that —I can give you the very words— 'No matter what fluctuations there might be on the exchange, you were prepared to accept then, or at any future time, Austrian crowns for any sterling or dollar investments which you might hold at not more than twenty-five thousand crowns to the pound'?

"You made that statement publicly at a time when crowns were at the rate of about twenty thousand to the pound, and when you persuaded me and my friends to trust in you. Now, crowns are at anything —one hundred and fifty thousand or one hundred and sixty thousand to the pound. Therefore, I have come to London to demand that you redeem those words!"

For the first time Otto Bernstorm's face showed signs of emotion. A black cloud of anger gathered on his brow.

"I have already said that you were mad!" he snarled. "But I think you are just a plain fool. I have already told you that the words I uttered on that occasion were merely out of politeness to those who were my hosts. Your common-sense must tell you that no man could be held to a statement of that sort.

"Do you expect me to hand over any sterling investments I might have, and accept from you twenty-five thousand crowns for each pound in value instead of the current rate? Such a mad procedure would put me in the bankruptcy court in a week!"

"Yet you expect us to stand the loss, and it matters not to you that some of us are already bankrupt, and through you! And I tell you here and now, Bernstorm we are not going to do it. Either you redeem the promise of those words, or I take other measures!"

"Then, let me advise you to take other measures, for I shall certainly not do any thing as mad as you propose! That is final!"

"Absolutely?"

"Absolutely! Now, will you be good enough to get out? I am busy!"

There was a dead silence for nearly a minute, while the man across the desk studied the financier. Then he said very quietly:

"By heavens! It is true; they are right! You are nothing but a common crook! Other measures —yes, I will take other measures now!"

With that his hand came out of the side-pocket of his coat, and the next instant Otto Bernstorm found himself gazing into the barrel of a heavy blue automatic pistol. He stiffened.

"I—I—" he began.

Crash! The weapon spoke just once, and as Otto Bernstorm whirled and fell to the floor from the impact of the heavy bullet the Magyar thrust the pistol back into his pocket, snatched up his hat, and, unlocking a side door, stepped out into the corridor.

Less than a minute later he was in Crosby Square, and a few

seconds after that the hurrying crowds in Bishopsgate Street had swallowed him.

Strangely enough the crash of the pistol in Otto Bernstorm's private room had not been heard by the clerks in the outer office, due, apparently, to the fact that there was a passage between the two offices, and also to the noise made by a steam derrick just outside in the square.

Therefore, it was not until Franklin returned some ten minutes later that he found his employer groaning on the floor, with a pool of blood rapidly spreading over the rich Persian rug. And with that discovery all became confusion in Otto Bernstorm's office.

The Third Chapter. A Shady Past —Familiar Features —What the Tape Told —What the Inspector Knew —"It was Edward Studdington" —Blake Plays a Lone hand —In Bernstorm's Office.

"WHAT do you make of this case, guv'nor?"

Blake looked up from an old volume of the "Index" in which he had been studying the Baker Street record of Otto Bernstorm.

"I don't make anything of it yet, Tinker. It is altogether obscure. There are two or three points about it which I find extremely puzzling."

"What are those, guv'nor?"

"Well, take for instance, the amount of bearer-bonds which were abstracted from Bernstorm's safe —exactly twenty thousand pounds in all. Yet, in the safe, quite as easily accessible, were further bonds totalling close to a hundred thousand pounds.

"Why didn't the thieves take those as well? Why were they satisfied with only a portion of the wealth which lay before them? The whole lot could be very easily disposed of.

"That is one point which puzzles me. Another is the fact that a certain amount in Austrian currency notes was left in place of the bonds. At present exchange, those currency notes are worth only a fraction of the value of the bonds, but it seems rather curious that the thieves took, firstly, the trouble to leave them, and, secondly, that they should choose just that amount.

"You see, Tinker, if they had been left out of sheer bravado —in other words, merely to mock Bernstorm —the purpose would have been served by leaving a much smaller quantity. But even at present exchange, five hundred million crowns is no small amount.

"It would take a little time and some trouble to get together that quantity in London, even though sellers are willing enough to part with them. The two circumstances, together with a certain something in Bernstorm's manner, make me think he has not been altogether frank with me.

"I will not go so far as to say that he suspects who it is who has robbed him, but, on his own confession, he dare not invite any publicity, and that looks bad. I haven't any idea just what his present financial activities are, but I shall have little difficulty in finding out in the City."

"It certainly seems funny why the thieves should leave those notes in place of the bonds," remarked Tinker, scratching his head.

"There doesn't seem any sense to it, guv'nor. Have you been able to get any ideas from Bernstorm's record?"

"No. I find that we have him entered up in the 'Index' all right. In fact, you yourself made the entry. It appears that he was one of the witnesses some years ago, at the scandal in which Sir Edward Studdington was convicted of fraud and sentenced to a long term on several charges.

"I had forgotten many of the details of that affair, but I recall them now. The whole thing was most unsavoury, and while Studdington paid the penalty, I remember that the judge remarked at the time that there were others, who, in his opinion, ought to have been in the dock instead of the witness-box.

"I fancy Bernstorm was mixed up in the promotion of the company more deeply than was generally known —he and the others to whom the judge referred. From what I can discover, he is the type of man who must have sailed pretty close to the wind on many occasions, and, likewise, the type who would have a good many things cropping up from the past. A man of that sort always leaves some wreckage in his wake."

"Well, sir, whoever nicked those bonds out of his safe certainly did a good job."

Blake nodded.

"A professional job, my lad. It is certain that a microphone was used, but beyond the faint marks of the attachment, there is absolutely nothing else to go upon. The most puzzling feature is how they managed to get into the house and out again. I cannot but believe that someone inside was a confederate."

Tinker smiled suddenly.

"I say, guv'nor, if this had happened a few years ago, I'd have said it had a good many features about it that looked like the work of an old friend of ours."

"What do you mean, Tinker?"

"Why, Mademoiselle Yvonne, guv'nor. That touch about leaving the notes was exactly the sort of thing she would have done."

Blake did not smile, as Tinker expected. Instead, he looked at the lad very thoughtfully, then he nodded his head slowly.

"Yes, you are quite right, Tinker. It is most certainly the type of thing Mademoiselle Yvonne would have done.

"With her there would have been a purpose in leaving the notes. What that purpose might be, we do not know. But it could not have been she, because we know that she has —er—"

"Reformed," put in Tinker with another grin, and Blake let it go at that.

"At the same time," he went on. "I don't know that there isn't the germ of an idea in your suggestion, my lad. Someone might have taken a leaf out of Yvonne's book. It is a possibility we shall bear in mind. By the way, do you happen to know if Mademoiselle Yvonne is in town?"

"I don't know, sir. Shall I telephone and find out?"

"No. Don't bother now. I want to telephone through to my broker to make some inquiries for me about Otto Bernstorm. Then we shall go on to the Venetia grill-room for lunch, where I promised to meet Colonel Foster and discuss that Chinese matter we have in hand."

As he finished speaking, Blake drew the telephone instrument towards him and gave the number of his broker. He explained what it was he wished to know, and then, when he had hung up the receiver, rose.

They drove through in the Grey Panther to the Venetia, where Blake descended and made his way into the bar, while Tinker parked the car in the middle of Piccadilly. On his way to the bar, Blake paused by the tape-machine and began idly running the paper slip through his fingers. He was scrutinising the latest prices of certain shares when the instrument began clicking, and he gazed through the glass to see what was coming up.

As the message was slowly spelled out, he bent closer, keenly interested to read the completion of the message.

The printing-wheel seemed to be in a particularly erratic condition that day, for it would write half a word then come to a pause with a loud, irritating buzz. At last, however, it completed the line, and when the paper roll had been spaced half a dozen times, indicating that the message was complete, Blake lifted the paper above the machine, and read:

"Otto Bernstorm, the financier, was shot at and severely wounded in his office this morning. His assailant escaped, and, although conscious, the financier was unable to give any description of him. The wounded man has been removed to his home, where, it is reported, the bullet had been successfully removed."

Blake gave a low whistle of surprise, and was just dropping the slip when Tinker came up. In silence he pointed out the message, which Tinker read quickly.

"Scott, guv'nor!" exclaimed the lad. "That is funny. Who do you suppose shot him, the same person who robbed his safe last night?"

"It is impossible to say," answered Blake. "We will look into it after lunch. Don't say anything before Colonel Foster. Here he comes now."

They went forward to meet the tall, thin, elderly man who was coming across the lounge, and, after a brief visit to the bar, all three descended to the grill-room for lunch.

During the meal Blake discussed the matter on which Colonel Foster had sought his advice —a case involving a technical point of Chinese usage, on which Blake was an expert. Blake did not spend much time over the coffee and liqueurs, for he was anxious to get first-hand particulars regarding the shooting of Otto Bernstorm.

The affair had followed so close on the heels of what had taken place the night before that it was impossible not to wonder if there was some very close connection between the two. As soon as they decently could, he and Tinker took their departure, and, as Tinker slumped into the seat behind the wheel. Blake said curtly:

"Drive to Upper Brook Street, Tinker."

On pulling into the kerb near Bernstorm's house, it was plain that there must be some truth in the report which Blake had read on the tape-machine, for just outside the kerb three cars were standing, and in one of them Blake recognised a driver from Scotland Yard.

The other two cars were typical of the sort used by professional men. Blake left Tinker in the Grey Panther and went up the steps. In response to his ring the door was opened by the butler whom he had interviewed that morning. As Blake stepped into the hall and the door closed after him, he said:

"I have just heard of the accident to Mr. Bernstorm. Is it serious?"

"I can't say, sir," answered the man "The doctors are with the master now. But Mr. Franklin, the master's confidential clerk, is in the library, sir. He is attending to everything for the present. Will you come along there?"

"Yes. I—"

Blake broke off as he caught sight of a figure descending the stairs. A moment later he saw that it was Inspector Thomas, of Scotland Yard. He waited until the inspector had reached the ground floor. As they shook hands the man from Scotland Yard said:

"What are you doing here, Blake? Did Bernstorm send for you?"

"No. I had a little business with him, and just heard a short while ago of the shooting. Have you seen him?"

"Yes. I have just come from his room. They have got the bullet out all right, and he is resting fairly easy."

"Is it serious?"

"Serious, but not dangerous, he will get over it all right. The bullet went too high to be fatal. It was either fired in a hurry or by a nervous hand, because, from the size of the wound, it must have been fired at very close quarters. And it was a .450 at that. It has smashed up his left shoulder considerably, and torn the muscles, but that is all."

"A close shave," remarked Blake. Then he looked at the inspector. "In the report on the tape it said that he didn't recognise his assailant. Is that true?"

The inspector gave a grunt.

"No one can tell whether it is true or not.

"As soon as I received official notice of the affair, I came on here. I have just seen Bernstorm, and have talked with him. He protests that he did not see his assailant distinctly, as he must have managed to enter the room quietly by a side door that leads into the corridor. He says that he was so engrossed over some papers that this might have been possible without attracting his attention.

"He says that the first thing he knew, he became aware that someone was standing on the other side of his desk. He thought it must have been one of his clerks. He looked up, and then saw that it was a stranger.

"Before he could speak, the man lifted a pistol and fired. That is all he remembers, except that he adds that there was something familiar about the man who shot him. After questioning him, he said that he was not certain enough to make a direct accusation, as the man his assailant reminded him of was in prison —or, at least, he supposed he was. I asked him for the name, and he gave it."

"What was the name? Are you at liberty to tell me?"

"Oh, I don't mind telling you, Blake. He named Edward Studdington, who was convicted of fraud some years ago, and sentenced to fifteen years."

"Yes, I remember the case quite well," answered Blake, although he did not mention the coincidence of his having come across that same name only two or three hours before. "Well, Studdington is in prison, isn't he?"

"That is the funny part of it. Studdington was released just a little over a week ago. It looks as if Bernstorm's recognition was no mistake. At any rate, it makes the case strong enough for us to throw out the net for Studdington."

"It certainly looks bad for him. I wonder if Bernstorm knew that Studdington had been released?"

"No. He had lost track of him entirely. Didn't I just tell you that he said his assailant reminded him of a man he had known years ago, but that it couldn't be he because he was in prison?"

"Ah, yes. Quite so. Well, I suppose you will get after Studdington?"

Inspector Thomas nodded.

"At once. I don't think you will be able to see Bernstorm. I had trouble enough persuading the doctors to let me talk to him. It was only because it was essential that we should get after his assailant that they permitted me to do so."

"I shall not try to see him now. I will have a talk with his secretary instead."

They shook hands, and while the inspector took his departure, Blake walked along the hall to the library. As he entered, a man rose from before Bernstorm's desk, and Blake gave him a swift appraisal. In that swift scrutiny he had catalogued Franklin perfectly.

"My name is Blake —Sexton Blake." he said, as he crossed the room. "I have had a certain matter in hand for Mr. Bernstorm. I heard an hour or so ago of what had happened. I was shocked at the news, and I am glad that it is not as serious as was at I first thought."

"Oh, yes, Mr. Blake," responded the other I nervously. "Er —I am in Mr. Bernstorm's confidence, and I am aware of the details of the matter which you had in hand. But —er— Mr. Bernstorm has changed his mind; he had changed it before the accident.

"He had already decided, Mr. Blake, that he would not go ahead with the investigation on which he sought your advice. He repeated the instructions to me just before they extracted the bullet from his shoulder. If you will be so good as to send in an account for the services you have already rendered, I shall be glad to forward you a cheque."

"Do I understand, Mr.—"

"Franklin is my name, sir."

"Do I understand, Mr. Franklin, that Mr. Bernstorm has cancelled the instructions which he gave me this morning?"

"Yes."

"You know what took place last night?"

"Yes. As I told you, I am in Mr. Bernstorm's confidence."

"Then am I to take it that Mr. Bernstorm wishes me to do nothing further regarding the theft of twenty thousand pounds in bonds from his safe?"

"Yes, that is so, Mr. Blake."

"Mr. Bernstorm is, of course, at liberty to do as he wishes in the matter, but it strikes me as rather —curious, Mr. Franklin. Do you happen to know anything about my profession, Mr. Franklin?"

"Er —no, sir; except that, of course, I have heard a great deal about you."

"Then you are not aware that sometimes— sometimes, Mr. Franklin —I proceed on an investigation without being retained?"

"I don't quite understand, sir."

"I mean that when I find a case that interests me, I sometimes complete my investigations whether I am retained or not. It is just a matter of professional satisfaction —shall I say? And this case happens to interest me."

"But —but Mr. Bernstorm wishes you to drop it, Mr. Blake. He was most emphatic on that point. I can assure you that he will not pay any fee beyond that already incurred."

Blake drew out his cigarette-case and abstracted a cigarette. When he had lighted it he pointed the end in the direction of the secretary.

"Mr. Franklin, the fees in a case do not matter in the slightest to me. I do not pursue my profession merely for gain. And when, as I have already told you once, I am called in on a case, I use my discretion whether I pursue it or not.

"It has no bearing on my actions whether my client changes his mind or not. My whole decision rests on whether the case holds interest for me. Well, Mr. Franklin, this case promises to be quite interesting, and therefore I shall use my own discretion as to whether I follow it up or not. I may or I may not. You can communicate that to your employer when he is well enough to hear it. I will wish you good-day."

With that Blake turned and strode towards the door, leaving the amazed secretary gazing after him dumbfounded.

Blake had descended the steps leading to the street, and was just crossing the pavement, when he caught sight of a neatly dressed young woman coming up the basement steps. There was something about her face that struck Blake as familiar, and suddenly he remembered that she was one of the maids whom he had questioned that morning.

She looked somewhat different with a small toque on instead of the white cap she had worn before; but Blake noticed that, as in the morning, she seemed prone to flush, for as her eyes met his her face crimsoned.

"Nervous temperament," thought Blake. "And yet she has a pleasant, frank face. I wonder why she seems nervous of me? Surely it can't be possible that she could have been the inside accomplice. She hasn't the earmarks of that type of person. Still, you never can tell."

The girl had turned, and was now walking briskly down the street. Blake watched her for a short distance, then as he stepped into the car he said:

"Hop out, Tinker! Follow that young woman and see where she goes. Be careful that she doesn't spot you. I am going into the City, and will then return to Baker Street. Meet me there."

Tinker was already out of the car, and, at Blake's last words, he started off down the street after the maid. Blake turned the Grey Panther, and, swinging round the corner, drove at a rapid pace towards Piccadilly.

From there he proceeded, by way of Charing Cross and the Embankment, to Ludgate Circus, and thence on to the Mansion House, where he passed through Threadneedle Street and so into Bishopsgate.

He did not drive the car into Crosby Square, but left it in Bishopsgate, and made his way in on foot. His objective was Otto Bernstorm's office, for, while he had not finally decided whether he would drop the case or not, he was curious to have a look at the office where the shooting had taken place.

On reaching the main office, he found most of the clerks still in an excited state over the affair. They were gathered together in little groups, talking it over, but at sight of Blake the conversation stopped as though by magic. Blake guessed shrewdly that orders had already been received from Franklin that there was to be no information handed out.

Blake selected a clerk and beckoned to him. He knew that if such an order had been issued, then his only way to overcome it was to strike so swiftly that the information he sought would be forthcoming before the brakes could be put on, so to say.

"My name is Sexton Blake," he said curtly to the clerk who approached. "I am handling a certain private matter for Mr. Bernstorm. I have just come from his house. I want to have a look at his private room. Please show it to me."

The mention of Blake's name gained the respect of the clerk at once; but, although he half turned towards the passage which led to the private room, he hesitated.

"Have you an authority from Mr. Franklin, Mr. Blake? You see, sir, we have received instructions—"

"That is for reporters," cut in Blake. "My time is valuable. Please do not force me to waste it."

"I—I— All right, sir. I suppose it is all right, although we have received very strict instructions."

Blake did not say whether it was all right or not, but, laying his hand on the gate that opened through the railing, stepped inside. The clerk, overcome by his dominant manner, meekly led the way along the passage to Otto Bernstorm's private room.

As he stepped inside, Blake's eyes sought first the desk at which Bernstorm had been sitting when the shot was fired, and then he glanced towards the second door that led out into the corridor. He strode swiftly across to this door and examined the lock.

"Bernstorm is a fool!" he thought, as he saw that it was a strong spring-lock fitted on the inside. "It would be impossible to enter this way without the right key, and even then it couldn't be done without, attracting the attention of anyone who sat at the desk.

"Bernstorm has lied to Inspector Thomas. Either he knew perfectly well who it was who entered and shot him, or else he is deliberately beclouding the issue."

Suddenly Blake turned and faced the clerk.

"How many visitors did Mr. Bernstorm have this morning before the shooting?" he snapped.

"Why, there was only one, sir."

"Did you see him?"

"Yes, sir. I showed him in —or, at least, it was I who informed Mr. Bernstorm that he was waiting."

"What do you mean?"

"The visitor wouldn't give his name, but insisted on seeing Mr. Bernstorm. As he was very persistent, I came to tell Mr. Bernstorm. He had at first refused to see the man, and instructed me to call a policeman if he refused to leave, but when he saw him he said it was all right."

"How long was he with Mr. Bernstorm?"

"I can't say, sir. He must have left by that door there. A great many visitors do so."

"I see. And was that the only visitor?"

"The only one who came through the main office, sir."

"Do many people come to see Mr. Bernstorm by this door that leads directly into the corridor?"

"Yes, sir —those with whom Mr. Bernstorm has private appointments."

"What was he like, this man you speak of? Was he fair or dark, old or young?"

"He was a big man, Mr. Blake, very dark, and a foreigner. I could tell that by his accent. He was dressed neatly, but in clothes that were very worn. He had a moustache, but no beard."

"You don't know his nationality?"

"No, sir; but as I closed the door I heard him speak in some foreign language to Mr. Bernstorm. It wasn't French or German or Spanish —that I know."

"Did he seem quite calm and normal?"

"He was quiet enough, but very determined to see Mr. Bernstorm."

"Do you think it was he who shot your employer?"

"That thought came to me at once as soon as we found Mr. Bernstorm. I asked him if it was this man, but he said it wasn't —that he had let him out before the shooting. He refused to say anything more then, as he was in such pain, but said he would give what information he could to the police."

"You did not hear the shot in the outer office?"

"No, sir. We heard nothing, and did not know Mr. Bernstorm had been shot until Mr. Franklin returned and found him."

"Do you know that Mr. Bernstorm says the shooting was done by a man who came into this room from the corridor?"

"I did not know that."

"Do you know if anyone else but Mr. Bernstorm carries a key of this door?"

"Mr. Franklin has one. But no one else has."

"Thank you. You might let me out this way. You need not tell Mr. Franklin how much you have told me. Just say that I insisted on viewing the office, and that you showed me in."

With that, Blake opened the door and made for the staircase. As he climbed back into the Grey Panther and headed for the West End, he muttered:

"Now, I wonder why Bernstorm said nothing to Inspector Thomas about that mysterious visitor? It would be interesting to know just what they talked about —Bernstorm with a man who wouldn't, give his name, and whom Bernstorm at first refused to see.

"You are a queer bird, Mr. Bernstorm. You may be telling the truth about this affair, but it doesn't look reasonable to me. I can't figure out how any man could open that door, even if he had the right key, and get across to the desk without attracting the attention of the person sitting at it, unless that person were deaf. And Otto Bernstorm is certainly not deaf."

Blake thought over the matter until he pulled up at the kerb in front of his house in Baker Street. He strode along to the consulting-room in a thoughtful mood, and so concentrated was his mind on the thing that was puzzling him that it was not until he had seated himself at his desk that he noticed a plain white envelope lying on the blotting-pad.

It bore no address, and he opined that someone must have dropped it through the letter-box in the door.

He slit the flap, and took out two small, folded bits of paper. He opened them up, then as he saw what they were his brow knit in puzzlement, for one appeared to be a clipping from a foreign newspaper, and the other bore a crude sketch which, a closer examination revealed, was undoubtedly intended to represent an oil-well derrick.

Blake laid down the sketch, and taking up the clipping, saw that it was from an Austrian paper. He was engaged upon making a free translation of the paragraph, when the consulting-room door flew open and Tinker dashed in. One look at his face told Blake that Tinker had news of import to impart.

"YES?" demanded Blake curtly.

Tinker tossed his cap aside.

"You certainly hit the nail on the head, guv'nor. It was a good thing I followed that maid."

"What happened?"

"She went straight to Mademoiselle Yvonne's offices in Oxford Street."

"What!"

"Fact sir. She was in a hurry, too. I had no trouble in keeping her in sight, for she didn't look round once. Then, when I saw her enter the building, I went after her. She went into mademoiselle's office, as I have said, and after about five minutes I went in, too.

"Well, guv'nor, she wasn't in the outer room, so that meant she was in the private office. I asked Miss Bryan to take my name in to Mademoiselle Yvonne. I thought while I was there I would put up a bluff, just to see what she would say. But she sent out word that she was sorry she was engaged and couldn't see me then.

"That struck me as queer, guv'nor, because usually she sees either of us, no matter what she is doing. It looks as if my shot wasn't so far off, after all."

Blake nodded and tapped the desk thoughtfully.

"Anything else?"

"Yes, sir. When she wouldn't see me, I went back to the street and kept watch on the entrance. I had been on the look out for about half an hour or so when Yvonne's car —the big touring car, not her two-seater drove in to the kerb. Alec was at the wheel. Then, a little later, Graves came out and spoke to Alec.

"A few minutes after that an elderly man appeared. He got into the back of the car and was no more than settled when Yvonne and the maid I followed from Upper Brook Street hurried out of the building and also got into the car. Then Graves took the seat beside Alec, and the car drove off at once. I couldn't very well follow, so I came on here to report."

"You speak of an elderly man. What did he look like?"

"Medium height, clean-shaven, snow-white hair, and very pale He was well-dressed in a quiet way, carried himself well, but sort of struck me as being a nervous sort. He ducked into the car like a scared rabbit."

Blake got up and took a volume of the "Index" from a shelf. He opened the volume and turned the pages until he came to the report of the trial of twelve years before, which he had studied only that morning.

Among the clippings which Tinker had pasted in were photographs of some of the chief actors in the drama, and among these was one of Sir Edward Studdington, the convicted man. Blake indicated the picture with his cigarette.

"Take a look at that, Tinker. Study it carefully. Allowing for an interval of some years, does it remind you of the man you saw today?"

Tinker bent over the book and studied the somewhat blurred photograph intently.

Then he nodded his head slowly.

"You have hit it, guv'nor. Take away the moustache in this picture, and add a few years, with the hair turned white —yes, sir, it must, have been Studdington. But what was he doing with Yvonne?"

Blake closed the book and pushed it aside. Then he reseated himself. For some time he sat gazing with knitted brow at the bare surface of the blotting pad on his desk. At last he spoke.

"I am beginning to think you spoke more truly than you thought," he said. "Studdington is out of prison —was released very recently. It hasn't taken him long to get mixed up with Otto Bernstorm, and in that Yvonne has had a hand as well.

"The evidence points to that very strongly, I am sorry. We don't know how deeply she is mixed up in the affair, but if she has allowed her quixotic ideas to govern her actions, she is treading on very dangerous ground."

"How do you mean, guv'nor?"

"Studdington is wanted for the attempted murder of Otto Bernstorm. Bernstorm has accused Studdington, and Scotland Yard is now looking for him.

"In aiding a fugitive from justice. Yvonne is playing with fire — whether the man is innocent or guilty."

"Is there any doubt of that, guv'nor?"

Blake shrugged.

"They must, of course, prove him guilty. But that should not seem difficult when Bernstorm states that he recognised his assailant as Studdington, or, rather, as a man who reminded him strongly of Studdington, although he believed Studdington to be still in prison.

"On top of that accusation, Scotland Yard is acting in the only way it can. Inspector Thomas has the matter in hand."

"But what about Yvonne, guv'nor?"

"I can't quite fathom that, Tinker. From what you have been able to discover, I am now convinced that my first theory was correct — the abstraction of the bonds from Bernstorm's safe and the substitution of the Austrian currency notes was carried through with the aid of someone inside the house.

"That someone must have been the maid whom you followed to Yvonne's offices. If that is so, then it means that Yvonne has conceived the whole scheme —that she is working in with Studdington. I can only infer that the motive must be one of revenge against Bernstorm over the old affair of the Consolidated Lands Estates scandal. But why Yvonne should mix up in it I can't imagine.

"She knows what happened in the past when she took matters into her own hands. She knows how extremely difficult it made things for all concerned. And yet it certainly looks as if she had again embarked upon the same sort of risky business."

Blake paused and lifted up the newspaper clipping and the rough sketch.

"If my deductions regarding these two pieces of paper are correct," he went on slowly, "not only has she done that, but she is already aware that we have been retained by Bernstorm, but is so sure of herself that she has taken the trouble to send these to me anonymously —that she is laughing at us."

"I don't understand, guv'nor."

"I will explain. You see this newspaper clipping? It is taken from an Austrian paper —date unknown. It is part of a statement made by Otto Bernstorm in Vienna about exchange. In it he makes a very reckless statement —a statement on which someone has acted. This is to the effect that so confident does he feel in the economic soundness of Austria that he is prepared to say that her exchange will not collapse, and that, so far as he is concerned, he is at all times ready to exchange any sterling or investments he may hold for Austrian currency at a rate not exceeding twenty-five crowns to the pound sterling.

"At the time he made the statement, so this clipping says, the exchange rate was about twenty-thousand crowns to the pound. Now it is round a hundred and thirty thousand crowns.

"But this is the curious part of it all, Tinker. Twenty thousand pounds in sterling bonds were taken from Bernstorm's safe last night. In their place was left a bundle of Austrian currency notes to the amount of five hundred million crowns.

"That sounds a colossal sum, but if we reckon it out, we find that it would be exactly the equivalent of twenty thousand rounds at the rate of twenty-five thousand crowns to the pound —or, in other words, it looks as if someone had taken Bernstorm at his word and had relieved him of twenty thousand pounds worth of bearer-bonds, and had left in their place an equivalent amount of Austrian currency at the rate he stated publicly he was at all times prepared to accept. Of course, he was only talking moonshine when he made that statement, but it has cost him dear. That is the first point.

"The second is this. It looks as if Yvonne and Studdington were mixed up together in this. I have a strong suspicion that the scheme has been more the fruit of Yvonne's brains than of Studdington's.

"Your instinct was not at fault this morning when you said the affair smacked very strongly of some of the things Yvonne did in the past. Further, this rough sketch here is, I take it, a derrick, and a mining derrick at that.

"We can go a step further and conclude that it is supposed to represent an oil-well derrick. What does that suggest? It suggests an oil-well as having some connection with the affair, and we know that the Consolidated Lands Estates was an oil-well promotion. Ergo, we come straight back again to Studdington."

"The way you put it, it certainly looks as if you are right, guv'nor. At the same time, if Studdington and Mademoiselle Yvonne were working together, and the taking of the bonds was their scheme to get even in some way with Otto Bernstorm, why did Studdington follow that up by shooting Bernstorm?"

"You have raised a good point there, Tinker, and I will try to answer it in what I think a logical way. To begin with, there may be several things to account for that. If Studdington was being guided by Yvonne, then we know that she would never have permitted the shooting.

"If Studdington did invade Bernstorm's office and try to kill him, then it must have been because he acted on his own initiative. He may have got out of Yvonne's control.

"It may be that he had expressed his determination to kill Bernstorm, and she may have persuaded him to abandon the idea for a time. Then, as I say, in brooding over things he may have rushed off, and carried out his intention without her knowledge.

"While she would condemn the shooting —I am sure of that — she may have determined to assist him to escape out of loyalty. That is always presuming that Studdington did the shooting. On the other hand, he may have had nothing to do with it at all."

"Do you really think that, sir?"

"Well, after I left you at Upper Brook Street, I drove to the City —to Bernstorm's offices, to be exact. I had a talk with one of the clerks there, and from what he told me I am very much inclined to think it quite possible that the shooting was done by someone else."

"But Bernstorm himself says it was Studdington, or that the man looked like Studdington. Why would he accuse Studdington if he didn't do it? Besides, from what Inspector Thomas told you, it seems that Bernstorm did not know that Studdington was out of prison."

"Ha! He says so, but how do we know that he spoke the truth when he made that statement? We don't. Bernstorm may have had several reasons for throwing suspicion on Studdington. He may have known that he was out of prison, and he may have feared him.

"It is a fact that immediately after the shooting Bernstorm was unable to give any description of his assailant. And yet, after he had been taken to his home he made the accusation. Why didn't he do so before?

"Why did he apparently remember what his assailant looked like after he had had a chance to think things over? Why did he allow such a period of time to elapse before giving the police a clue? Was it because he has falsely accused Studdington? Is he deliberately shielding someone else? If so, then what is his motive? Is he afraid that if this someone else should be arrested, certain things will be made public that he wishes to be kept secret?

"From his own statements to me, I know that he is mixed up in several secret deals, which were sufficient to cause him to refuse to send for the police when his safe was robbed. Then isn't it possible that these same matters may have a bearing on the shooting and the identity of his assailant? I may see those points more clearly when I have discovered one thing."

"What is that, guv'nor?"

"When I know just when Otto Bernstorm made the accusation against Studdington. Did he make that accusation before or after the doctors had told him his wound was not dangerous? In other words, did he make it while he still feared death, or after he had been assured that there was no real danger?"

"By Jove! You seem to have thought of every point, guv'nor. What will you do now?"

"If we act on Otto Bernstorm's wishes we will do nothing. Through his confidential clerk he has requested me to drop the case."

"Drop it!" exclaimed Tinker, in amazement. "For goodness' sake, why?"

Blake shrugged.

"That is another one of the little mysteries about this business, my lad. I don't know why."

"And will you do so?"

"As far as acting for Otto Bernstorm —Yes. As far as following up a few points for my own private satisfaction —no. And, besides, Tinker, there is the question of Yvonne's participation in this. We don't know how deeply she is mixed up in it, but while Scotland Yard is seeking to extend their hospitality to Studdington, she is playing a dangerous game in assisting him to evade arrest.

"And, in addition, there it the mockery of these two slips of paper, my lad. We shall see if we can apply the adage in this instance —that he who laughs last laughs best.

"Now then, to get down to business. If, as it seems, Yvonne is assisting Studdington to evade arrest, then of one thing we may be sure —she will lose no time in getting him out of the metropolitan area.

"That means they will make for some place in the country, where Studdington will lie low until Yvonne tries to straighten things out. I cannot conceive of a more likely place for their purpose than Graves' place in Hampshire.

"It is quiet, and, as Yvonne can trust all her servants and employees not to talk, it would be the safest spot for the time being.

"She might, if necessity arose, try to smuggle him aboard the Fleur-de-Lys, and then to land him in either Greece or Turkey, as extradition agreements with those two countries are non-operative at the present time.

"But we shall try to checkmate her there. To that end you will take the Grey Panther, and go down into Hampshire. I need not impress upon you the need for circumspect action. You can look things over down there, and it won't take you long to discover whether Studdington is staying with Graves or not. But what you have to do then will not be so easy."

"What is that, sir?"

"You will, by hook or by crook, force Studdington into the Grey Panther, and bring him here."

Tinker whistled.

"That is a tall order, guv'nor! Do you mean I am to force him to come —to kidnap him?"

"If necessary —yes. By the time you have carried out your part of the plan, I hope to have achieved something here in town. There is a certain line I shall follow up. On my success in that direction depends our next move.

"If I succeed, and if I am able to confirm a theory which I have formed, then Studdington will be at liberty to do as he chooses, for, under my new instructions, I shall not communicate any solution of the robbery to Otto Bernstorm. On the other hand, Yvonne must be brought up with a round turn before she gets on the wrong side of Scotland Yard. And, finally, I am curious —distinctly curious about certain phases of Mr. Otto Bernstorm's activities.

"Use your own judgment, my lad. You can only tell how you must act when you have looked the ground over. But follow your instructions to the letter —bring Studdington back with you."

"What if Mademoiselle Yvonne and Graves object?" asked Tinker, with a grin.

Blake's jaw set.

"You will not let that interfere with what you have to do," he said coldly.

"And the maid?"

"You need not worry about her. If we want her, we know where we can lay our hands on her. We can always reach her through Yvonne, for she is apparently under her protection. I suggest you fill up with petrol, and start to-night. The sooner you can strike the more chance you have of success."

"Very good, sir!"

With that Tinker made for his room to pack a small bag, while Blake turned his attention back to the two slips of paper.

" What has happened, Stella ? " asked Yvonne quiet'y. " Something has upset you, but you must not be frightened." " It's about Mr. Bernstorm, miss." " You mean about the shooting, Stella ? " " Yes, miss." (*Chapter* 5.)

BLAKE'S deductions, which he had made from the rather scanty material of Tinker's report, had been closer to truth than even he himself guessed.

While he did not know that very shortly after his departure from the house in Upper Brook Street that morning, Stella Bentley, the maid, had slipped out to telephone to Yvonne that Sexton Blake had been sent for by her master, and while he did not know that this information had inspired Yvonne to send him the two slips of paper anonymously, it had not taken him long to link up the other points as soon as he had heard Tinker's report.

Now, although Blake was very dubious of Otto Bernstorm's honesty in naming Studdington as his assailant, he had no real proof that the accusation had been falsely made.

Nor had he at present anything to follow up which might give him a clue to the truth other than the question he proposed putting to one of the doctors who had operated on Bernstorm. To Blake's mind the answer to that question was most important.

And had he been able to overhear the conversation which had taken place in Yvonne's private room while Tinker kept watch in the street below, he would have realised its importance even more fully.

Yvonne had hardly more than despatched the envelope to Baker Street —she had sent it in a spirit of sheer mischievousness —when Miss Bryan had opened the door to admit Sir Edward Studdington.

One glance at his face told her something was wrong, and without any preliminaries she motioned him into the big chair by the desk. Her visitor was obviously labouring under some strong emotion —fear, Yvonne diagnosed it —and he was still trying to conquer his emotion and speak when Graves came in. He gave a quick glance towards Studdington, then, turning to Yvonne, said: "has he told you?"

Yvonne shook her head.

"Sir Edward has just this moment come in. I am waiting to hear what has upset him."

The latter had now succeeded in controlling his agitation. "You have heard, then?" he said, looking at Graves.

Graves nodded.

"I read it on the tape at the club."

"What is it?" asked Yvonne quickly. "Please tell me at once what has happened!"

It was Graves who answered her.

"Otto Bernstorm has been shot and seriously wounded," he announced.

"Shot and wounded!" echoed Yvonne. "When did it happen? And where?" And as she asked the questions her gaze went swiftly to Studdington.

He shook his head.

"I know what you are thinking," he said, in a voice that trembled. "But I know nothing about it. I swear that is the truth. I only know what the tape says, and what I read in the first editions of the evening papers. It happened in his office."

"Do they know who did it?"

"Apparently not. The tape and the papers gave only the bare statement."

Yvonne looked at Graves thoughtfully. A little crease of anxiety appeared between her brows, for her quick mind had jumped at once to the danger this latest occurrence held for them. Through Stella Bentley she knew that Otto Bernstorm had called in Sexton Blake over the affair of the missing bonds, and she knew that with Blake employed on the case he would be bound to lose no time in following up the shooting.

She regretted now that she had sent the slips of paper to Blake, for where before she had been more amused than anything else at the prospect of Blake eventually discovering that she was behind the substitution of the Austrian currency notes for the bonds, and had been prepared, if cornered, to make a clean breast of things to him, the shooting of Bernstorm put a very different complexion on matters.

Not that she doubted Studdington's word. He had assured her that he knew nothing of the attempt on Bernstorm's life, and she believed him.

It was obvious that it had upset him greatly. But what Yvonne considered was the effect it would have on their campaign against the financier. As far as she had been able to find out through Stella Bentley, Bernstorm had not notified the police of his loss, but had contented himself with turning the inquiry over to Sexton Blake.

But the shooting would automatically pass into the hands of the police, and it would not be long before they would find out that Sexton Blake was already engaged on an inquiry that affected Bernstorm.

Thus it must follow, Yvonne opined, that once Scotland Yard was in touch with Blake, it was highly probable that whatever information Blake possessed would be placed at the disposal of the Yard. That is, if Blake should consider that the shooting might have been done by the same people who raided Bernstorm's safe.

While Yvonne had had little fear that Bernstorm would make a public outcry about his financial loss —she had discovered enough about his financial activities to cause her to think that —she knew any linking up of the two affairs meant, at the very least, considerable publicity and some very inconvenient police quizzing.

In fact, if Scotland Yard ever struck the truth about the bonds, and could persuade Bernstorm to make a charge, things would look pretty bad for them all.

These were the thoughts that were troubling her when once more the door opened. This time Miss Bryan announced that Stella Bentley had come, and stated that she must see Mademoiselle Yvonne at once. Yvonne gave instructions for the housemaid to be admitted, and a moment later a very frightened girl was standing before her. She grew calmer under Yvonne's cool smile.

"What has happened, Stella?" asked Yvonne quietly. "Something has upset you, but you must not be frightened. You know that I promised you you had nothing to fear, and I will keep my promise. You may speak freely in front of these gentlemen. They are in my confidence in this matter."

"It's —it's about Mr. Bernstorm, miss."

"You mean about the shooting, Stella?"

"Yes, miss. They brought him home, and the doctors have been there. There was a police inspector, too, miss. That is why I came to tell you as soon as I could. I —I listened to what they said, and then Mr. Sexton Blake came and talked with the inspector."

"Ah, that is important, Stella! Did you hear what the inspector and Mr. Blake said?"

"Not all, miss. But I did hear the inspector say that they knew who had done the shooting, and the police are after him now."

"Did he mention the name?" asked Yvonne sharply.

"Yes, miss. It was Stubbington or Studdington —something like that. I couldn't catch it very clearly."

A dead silence followed the girl's announcement. She could scarcely have created more consternation if she had dropped a bomb in the room. And then, before Yvonne could deal with this new phase of the affair there came a knock at the door, and Miss Bryan entered. It was then that she announced that Tinker had called and wished to see Mademoiselle Yvonne.

The reply that Yvonne sent out to Tinker is already known. Yvonne had very good reasons for avoiding a meeting with anyone from Baker Street, and she had a shrewd idea that Tinker's visit could only be connected in some way with the matter which was now assuming so many disquieting phases. When Miss Bryan had gone, Yvonne looked towards Studdington.

"This news is serious," she said slowly. "But even so, they can't convict you of something you haven't done."

Sir Edward had gone even whiter than the dead prison pallor made him appear. "But —but that is just the point!" he stammered. "The papers say the shooting took place just before mid-day.

"I was in the City at that time. I had gone to have a look at my old offices, and I must have been in Bishopsgate Street just about that hour. I —I haven't any alibi. There is no one I could call to prove where I was when the shooting occurred. But why —why has he accused me? I swear to you, mademoiselle, that I have not been in Bernstorm's offices to-day."

"And I have said that I believe you," rejoined Yvonne promptly. "But this certainly complicates matters. Let me think. Sit down Stella."

With that Yvonne lighted a cigarette, and smoked in silence for some minutes, while she turned over in her mind these new developments. Why the accusation had been made against Studdington she did not even attempt to guess.

That it had been made was the cold fact she had to deal with, and if it should be impossible to bring proof that he had not been near Bernstorm's offices when the shooting occurred, then it was going to be extremely difficult to make any jury believe that he was innocent, in the face of a direct accusation by the wounded financier for that Bernstorm had made the accusation Yvonne did not doubt for a single moment. The why would have to wait until later.

But it never occurred to her to desert Studdington in this new trouble that had descended upon him. The fact that he had previously served a long term in prison would go against him, and that record, on top of a direct accusation by Bernstorm, would mean that his conviction on the charge of shooting with intent to kill would be inevitable.

And yet, Yvonne knew that he spoke the truth when he denied all knowledge of the affair. Her belief, however, would not influence a judge and jury who must deal with the evidence submitted to them. And what judge or what jury would acquit, in the face of Bernstorm's sworn testimony that his assailant was Studdington?

No British judge and no British jury, she knew, for British law insists upon cold facts. Without very strong proof, how would they know that the "facts" in this case were false?

Thus Yvonne struggled with the problem. If a hue and cry was already started for Studdington, then there was little time to act. For one fleeting moment it came to her that her best step would be to get in touch with Sexton Blake at once, and ask him what she had better do —to make a clean breast of everything to him, and leave it to him to find a way out of the tangle.

But then came the thought that he might not be quite so ready as she to believe Studdington's statement, and, further, her pride would not let her seek help from him whom she had mocked only an hour or so before. At last she looked up.

"We shall have to get Sir Edward out of London at once," she said. "I think your place in Hampshire would be best for the present, uncle. Then I shall try and straighten things out. Sir Edward must not be arrested now. We must keep him hidden until further evidence comes to light, or until we can find some means of putting up a case against Bernstorm's accusation that will hold water.

"You, too, Stella. I think had better go into the country for the present. If Mr. Sexton Blake is engaged on this matter, then he is bound to discover, sooner or later, that we had assistance inside the house. I will make myself responsible for your future. We will get started as soon as Alec can get the car here."

Graves nodded his agreement, and Yvonne drew the telephone instrument towards her. She got through to her flat at Queen Anne's Gate, and gave the necessary instructions to Anna. Then she called in Miss Bryan, and with cool efficiency wound up several outstanding items of work.

54

By the time she had finished Alec had arrived with the car, and that is how, a few minutes later, Tinker, who was on watch m the street below, saw the party leave Oxford Street for an unknown destination.

Tinker left the shelter of the tree, and approached the brilliantly lighted window of the dining-room. He stopped, and, with infinite caution, lifted his head and peered over the sill. Inside he saw Mademoiselle Yvonne, Graves, and the elderly man whom Yvonne had rushed away from earlier in the day. (*Chapter 6*.)

Sir Edward Studdington staggered back as he flung the door open at the sight of the formidable-looking figure that faced him. "One yelp," cautioned Tinker, "and I will drill you!" (*Chapter 6*)

The Sixth Chapter. The Village Inn —At Graves' House —Seen Through the Window —Inside —A Surprise for Sir Edward — Kidnapped.

IT was something over two hours after the departure of Yvonne and her party for the country that Tinker got away in the Grey Panther. He knew the way well enough, for since Graves had taken over the sporting property in Hampshire both he and Blake had been there on several occasions. Once clear of the suburbs, he went all out, despite the frequency of suspected police-traps, for Blake had impressed upon him the necessity of finding out definitely if it was to Graves' place that the fugitives had gone.

If Blake's theory on that point should prove incorrect, then Tinker had instructions to communicate with Baker Street without delay, so that Blake might start at once to locate the Fleur-de-Lys, Yvonne's yacht.

Tinker knew he had little hope of overtaking the other car unless they sustained a breakdown or should stop on the way for refreshment. But he did not think either contingency likely. In the first place Yvonne's cars were always kept too well tuned up by Alec, the chauffeur; and, the second, he opined that Yvonne would not risk attracting undue attention to her party by stopping at any place en route.

And it proved eventually that Tinker right, for he arrived at the little village about a mile from Graves estate without once sighting the others.

When Tinker had left London a slight drizzle had been falling from the leaden clouds which had been threatening all day, and as he got deeper into the country the drizzle turned to a steady downpour, which had all the looks of having set in for the night by the time he reached his destination.

He had chosen the little village as his base, as it was the nearest hamlet to Graves' place, and still was far enough away for him to keep under cover if necessary.

It was a very small village, with a single inn; but Tinker knew, from previous experience, that he would find real comfort, a pleasant fire, and good food there. Nor was he disappointed.

When he had driven the Grey Panther into the tiny, one-car garage, and made his way into the inn, he found a cheerful log fire burning in the cosy little parlour. And when he had thrown aside his wet motoring garments, the glass of hot spiced ale which the buxom innkeeper brought him made Tinker think of the famous spiced ale of the old English coaching days —now, alas! a thing of the past.

The woman had seen Tinker when he had been at the inn with Blake; but she had no idea who the lad really was, and Tinker had little fear of his identity getting out through her, as it was very rarely that any of the stable or grounds hands from Graves' came to the inn. They preferred to patronise the inns at a larger village about a mile and a half on the other side of the estate.

He found that she could provide him with a hot supper inside the half hour, and that she had a room available. When he had drunk his ale and his chilled body had felt the warmth of it, he rose, and followed the boots to the room which had been prepared for him.

It was a large, low chamber, with heavy ancient rafters that had been hewn in the days of long ago, when the best of the forest went into the building of the houses of England. On the ruddy-hued tallboy two candles burned in tall brass sconces, and in the wide fireplace another cheerful log fire was burning, with a plentiful supply of dry wood close at hand when needed.

The bed was an enormous four-poster, against which the sheets and pillows gleamed whitely, with an inviting look. Tinker yawned, and looked about him longingly. He was half tempted to turn in without more ado; but he had to thrust the idea from him, for he still had work to do that night.

He promised himself, however, that on his return to the inn he would lose little time in tumbling into the great bed.

Supper was on the table when he descended, and the appetising odour did not belie its quality. Chicken and home-cured bacon, thick slices of home-made bread with great chunks of yellow butter, and, to top off, a brimming jug of milk, with clotted cream and preserves. Tinker gave a contented sigh as he rose and made his way back to the parlour; nor did he see the pleased amazement of his buxom hostess as she regarded the effects of his attack on the table.

A short pipe before the fire in the parlour, then Tinker rose and reached for his coat. Slipping this on and belting it about him, he drew his leather motoring cap well down over his eyes. In the outer pocket of his coat he thrust his automatic, and then, with a brief word to the innkeeper that he expected to be about an hour, he opened the outer door and plunged into the driving rain.

The village street was deserted, and on each side the gutters ran nearly full with the rain-wash. Here and there a light showed that some cottager was still up, or the lights had been left as a guide for those who were at the inn, and the murmur of whose voices he had heard as he sat in the parlour. In a few minutes he had reached the outskirts, and was stumbling along the road which led towards Graves' place.

He took no precaution, for he knew he had little chance of meeting anyone from the estate. It would be time enough when he entered the grounds. And, as a matter of fact, he covered the whole distance to the main gates without meeting a single soul.

He knew that he had no lodgekeeper to avoid, and he knew, further, that the big iron gates would probably be locked. But counting on finding the small gate unlocked.

This was set in one of the larger gates, and after a few minutes' fumbling about, Tinker found that he was right. He opened it carefully and slipped inside the grounds. He could see no sign of a light at the house; but he recalled that the main driveway took a broad turn between the main gates and the house, and realised that the trees which lined the drive must obscure the house from view even in the daytime, although for the moment he could not quite recall whether this was so or not.

A few minutes proved that it was so, for as he stole cautiously up the drive, keeping in beneath the dripping trees at one side, he at last caught sight of a light burning, he thought, in a room on one of the upper floors. The trees opened out somewhat now, although that fact did not make it any easier for Tinker to see.

The rain had grown heavier, if anything, and time after time he went sprawling over a projecting root or branch into the sodden grass. Going on his previous knowledge of the place, he gradually bore off to the left until he knew he ought to come out at one side of the mansion, and not far from the big brick wall that shut off the kitchen garden.

It was his idea to prospect from the shelter of this wall. It seemed to take an infernally long time to find it, but he had not made sufficient allowance for the ground he was losing owing to the erratic course the darkness forced him to follow.

He had come to a pause beneath a tree, and was debating if he should change his plans, when, in a room on the ground floor, he saw a sudden glow against one of the dark windows. That settled him. Leaving the shelter of the tree, he took the oblong glow as a mark, and a few minutes later knew he had reached the side of the house which was his objective.

There he saw another glow —or, rather, a rectangle of clear bright light —and that light gave Tinker his exact whereabouts. A few yards from him he now discerned the brick wall, and from this, he knew the bright light must be shining in the dining-room.

He slipped across until he was close beside the wall, and, keeping one arm against it, went slowly forward towards the lighted window. There was no balcony, but the window was a wide one with a broad sill; and, even though the rain was driving down, the lower sash had been lifted a few inches to permit the rain-cooled night air to filter into the room.

On the other side of the sash lace curtains waved gently under the draught. Tinker went forward, crouching, until his fingers encountered the stonework just beneath the sill. Then he stopped, and with infinite caution, lifted his head until he could see over the lower frame of the sash.

As he peered through the lacy pattern of the curtain his lips moved in soundless satisfaction, for gathered at the table he saw Mademoiselle Yvonne, Graves, and the white-faced, elderly man whom Yvonne had rushed away from Oxford Street that day, and who Tinker now knew was none other than Sir Edward Studdington.

The latter looked worried and harassed, and even the usually imperturbable Graves had an expression of mild anxiety on his face. But Yvonne looked as cool and self-possessed as ever, and seemed to be thoroughly enjoying the meal.

From time to time the murmur of their voices reached him, but the racket of the driving rain made it impossible for Tinker to hear what they were saying. He watched while a maid entered the room and placed a dish on the table; then, when she had departed, he backed away from the window and moved along the wall until he was out of the penumbra of light.

"Good old guv'nor!" he muttered. "Perhaps he didn't shoot the works this time all right. Hit it bang in the middle. His mind was just about two jumps ahead of Yvonne's. Like me, they were hungry when they arrived, only it has taken longer to get the meal ready. And I'll bet they won't stay up late to-night.

"Even if Graves stays smoked away down here for a few days, it's a certainty, as the guv'nor thought, that Mademoiselle Yvonne will hit the road for town to-morrow morning.

"That first light I saw must have been upstairs. Why wouldn't it be in the room being prepared for Studdington? The second light on the ground floor, I know now, was in the study. That means they will probably have coffee and cigarettes served in there after supper.

"H'm! 1 won't, bet on it, but, if I remember rightly, the room upstairs where I saw the light was the same room occupied by the guv'nor when he was down here just before the Winfield Handicap. It would be natural to put Sir Edward in there. I wonder— Scott! I'll have a shot at it! The light in the study must have been turned on by one of the servants who was seeing that the room was all right before they came in for coffee. I'll take a look-see!"

With that, Tinker made his way back along the wall, and then, when there was no danger of being seen from the dining-room, he crossed the grass swiftly, swung round the corner of the house, and kept on close to the wall until he came to the window where he had seen the glow of light.

The window was only a black patch now, however, and as his fingers went along the sill, Tinker felt with one free hand for something which he carried in the inside pocket of his motor-coat. He drew it forth, and, had there been any light, one might have seen that it was a thin strip of highly polished steel, one end of which had been tapered down to a keen edge.

Bringing this into use, Tinker thrust the edge beneath the sash and pressed gently.

At first the sash did not move, and he thought the catch must be fastened, but when he increased the pressure somewhat, he felt the frame give suddenly, and a moment later he was able to insinuate his fingers beneath the sash.

Then he thrust the strip of steel back into his pocket, and, working with both hands, forced the sash up and up until the space was large enough to admit his body. Now he stood with his head bent, listening intently.

His groping fingers came in contact with heavy curtains, which he separated a few inches. As he did so, he saw the cheerful glow of a fire, and on a table near was a tray containing cups. It was as he had thought— the light he had seen had been when one of the servants was placing the tray in the room.

When a cautious survey told him that the room contained no human occupant. Tinker threw a leg over the sill and slipped inside. He closed the window after him, and pulled the curtains back into place.

Willy-nilly, he was irrevocably committed now to the plan he had formed while he crouched outside the dining-room, and he knew that he must move with the greatest circumspection, for any moment might bring discovery, and that meant disaster to Blake's plans.

From what he had been able to see through the dining-room window, he knew that Yvonne and the others would be at the table for some little time to come, for they appeared but to have begun the meal.

But that did not lessen the risk of discovery, for he knew the servants would still be about, and more particularly on the upper floor, where they would be busy getting rooms ready against the unexpected arrival of Yvonne and the others.

Tinker stole across the room until he reached the door leading out into the hall. He knew that, immediately beyond, the hall stretched away to the front of the house, where it broadened into a large, square entrance lobby containing a big, old-fashioned fireplace. He knew further that from this entrance lobby the main staircase led to the floor above, and that was his objective if he could run the gauntlet.

He dared not stand too long in one spot, for although he had given his overcoat a shake before climbing through the window, it was still dripping water, and even in the subdued light cast by the fire Tinker could see that his passage across the room had been marked by a succession of wet splotches.

He knew these would certainly be seen by Yvonne, but he trusted to luck that she would conclude they had come there by the carelessness of Graves or Studdington when they had first arrived. Therefore, after listening for a few moments, he opened the door and stepped out into the ball.

At the far end a light was burning, but where Tinker stood it was in shadow. Keeping back against the wall, he listened again, but when he neither heard nor saw any sign of the servants he started towards the staircase at the other end.

Reaching it, he swung round by the newel post and began to

mount. He had reached the turning about half-way up, when suddenly he heard a door close on the floor beneath. He hesitated for a second, then as the sound of footsteps came along the hall, he leant forward, and caught a fleeting glimpse of a woman's skirts.

From the white apron he knew it was one of the maids. The next instant he was round the bend of the staircase, and, covering the steps two at a time, reached the first floor.

He sped as silently as possible along the wide corridor until he reached the door of the apartment which Sexton Blake had occupied on a previous visit to the place, and in which he was sure he had seen a light as he made his way through the grounds.

There was no time for uncertainty now, for he could distinctly hear the maid humming a tune of some sort as she mounted the stairs. If he should find another servant inside the room Tinker knew the game would be up, and that his only course would be to get past the maid, down the stairs, and away before she could give the alarm.

He opened the door even as he turned the handle, was inside in a single stride; then he closed the door and stood with his back against it.

Came the sound of footsteps in the hall outside. For one tense moment Tinker thought they had come to a pause just outside the door against which he leant, but he breathed easier as he heard them pass on.

The slam of a door followed, and with that Tinker reached along the wall until he found the switch.

In the flood of light he gazed about the room he had entered so unceremoniously. He had chosen rightly, he saw at the first glance, for he at once recognised it as the apartment which Blake had occupied. But whether it was the one which had been set aside for Studdington he had yet to discover.

There was no luggage about the room which would serve as a clue, for, of course, none had been brought in the car from London. Studdington, Tinker opined, would be lent what he needed by Graves.

As a matter of fact, Tinker saw an array of toilet articles laid out on the dressing-table, and on the bed were pyjamas. But a brief examination of the former revealed that they bore Graves' crest, while on the pyjamas was embroidered his monogram.

Tinker next turned his attention to a door on the left, which he knew opened into a large wall cupboard. And there he came upon the clue he sought, for, in addition to several masculine garments which he concluded must belong to Graves, he saw hanging the raincoat and soft hat which Studdington had been wearing when Yvonne's car had departed from her offices in Oxford Street.

Tinker stood regarding the interior of the closet for a few moments, then he gave a nod of quick decision. Turning, he strode back to the switch, and the next instant the room was plunged into darkness.

Cautiously he felt his way back to the closet. Just inside the door he removed his own overcoat and stuffed it well back out of sight behind some of the other garments. Then he slipped his automatic in the side pocket of his coat, and from an inner pocket took something which he placed in the other side-pocket, ready for instant use.

That done, he closed the door gently, and felt about until he had worked himself well in behind the hanging garments. He had no idea how long his vigil would last, and as he thought he would be fairly safe until Studdington appeared, he squatted down on his heels and set himself patiently to wait.

As a matter of fact, it was over an hour later when Tinker heard a door close and then footsteps in the room beyond the cupboard door.

"Studdington," he muttered, and came to his feet silently. "I'll give him about five minutes, in case Graves should come along to speak to him; then I'll make a move. After that —well, I shall have to act as circumstances force me. But one thing is dead certain —Sir Edward Studdington is in for one of the biggest surprises of his life in the next few minutes."

Working cautiously. Tinker drew out the object which he had placed in the left side pocket of his coat, and carefully adjusted it over his face.

In the light it would have been revealed as a mask of an extraordinary type for instead of being dead black, as is usually the case, it was of black and white, made in a series of alternating, wavy lines which gave the wearer a particularly sinister appearance

Next, he drew out his automatic, and, with that in his hand, stole towards the door. With his finger on the handle, and just in the act of turning, he stiffened, for a footfall sounded immediately outside.

The next second the door was pulled and Sir Edward Studdington staggered back with a gasp at the sight of the ferocious looking figure which faced him, pistol pointing straight at his heart.

"One yelp out of you, and I will drill you!" snarled Tinker hoarsely. "Back up! Go on — more, more! There! Stand just where you are, and remember what I told you!"

There was no means for Studdington to know that the sinister-looking individual who threatened him with the pistol was throwing a cold bluff, and that, had he raised the alarm, the other would have made a leap for the door.

To begin with, Tinker's appearance was enough to put fear into the most hardened; and more so in the case of a man like Studdington, whose nerves were ragged after years in prison, and who was in a state of terror at the prospect of again going behind grim prison walls under the accusation Bernstorm had made against him.

Therefore, he obeyed Tinker to the letter, and when the latter ordered him to put his hands behind him, he did so.

Tinker worked swiftly then. First, he jerked the cord from a dressing-gown which had been thrown over the end of the bed, and with this he bound Studdington's wrists securely.

That done, he forced his prisoner into a chair, making him sit sideways. He searched about until he found some silk handkerchiefs in a drawer, and with these proceeded to gag his man. He was just on the point of securing them in place, when suddenly he paused as a knock came at the door. With a single jerk, Tinker had the handkerchiefs out of Studdington's mouth, and, bringing his pistol up, pressed the end of the barrel against the other's temple.

"Ask who it is!" he commanded, with his lips close to Studdington's ear.

The other, terrified that his assailant would shoot at the slightest provocation, made an effort to speak, then, in a quavering voice, did as he was bid. In reply came a voice which Tinker recognised only too plainly as Graves'.

"Is there anything else you would like?" he called.

"Say 'No'!" hissed Tinker. "And keep your voice steady, if you don't want to be drilled!"

Studdington obeyed, and Tinker stood waiting tensely, watching the handle of the door until he heard a mutter from Graves, and then his footsteps passing along the hall. Tinker breathed easier then, for it meant that Graves was on his way to retire. That would indicate, he reasoned, that the whole household would have done the same —a condition of things he knew he must wait for.

But he did not relax his care on this account. He proceeded in a businesslike way to gag his prisoner, and, when that was done, sat down on the bed facing him, the pistol held in full view for Studdington to see.

Thus a half hour rolled by, then an hour. Not once did Tinker permit himself to relax, nor did he pay any attention to the puzzle expression in his prisoner's eyes.

He knew that Studdington was trying fathom the reason for the attack on him. Tinker knew he was all at sea to explain it, and it was part of the lad's purpose to keep him puzzled until he had him safely out of the house. He knew only too well that if Studdington guessed for single moment that it had all been inspired by the accusation made by Otto Bernstorm, he would risk everything to attract Graves' or Yvonne's attention. And that, Tinker also knew would spell disaster for him.

He had seized upon each thing as it had come; he had, by sheer daring, carried himself through to a point that he had scarcely anticipated being able to reach in less than two or three days, and he was determined to run his luck out, and, to use his own expression, "shoot the works."

If he failed, now that he had played part of his hand, he knew he would not have the ghost of a show afterwards. Yvonne would take good care to see to that. Therefore, while he was impatient to get away, he forced himself to wait until there could be no question that the household had retired.

When he felt this must be so, he slipped off the bed, and, bending over his prisoner, said:

"Now we are going to leave this room, and the house. Why I have come here for you, you will know in good time. But, understand, you are coming with me, and any interference is going to make me start pulling this trigger." (Which Tinker meant, although he did not add that he would shoot high if he did start.) "It's up to whether you start things or not. Now, sit there until I get your coat and hat! You will need them, for we travel fast and we travel far to-night."

With that he brought the other's coat and hat from the cupboard, and when Studdington had stood up, Tinker threw the coat over his shoulders and buttoned it into position.

Then, when he had crushed the soft hat on the other's head, he got his own raincoat and cap. Donning these, he walked back to his prisoner and grasped his arm.

"Now, listen!" he hissed. "We walk out of this room and along the hall to the stairs. See that you do not make a noise. If you do, you can take it from me that there is going to be the finest shooting racket out there that you ever imagined. You will walk as I guide you. Now, come on!"

With that, Tinker pushed his prisoner along to the door. He stood there for a moment, listening. Not a sound broke the stillness, so, reaching out, he switched off the light. Jamming the barrel of his automatic into Studdington's back, he opened the door and guided the other through.

His prisoner stood docilely enough while he closed the door, then, at a slow, cautious pace, Tinker and his charge started along the hall.

Tinker had the lie of the place in his mind well enough, but in the darkness it was difficult to judge distance exactly, and it seemed an eternity before his groping hand came into contact with the curve of the balustrade at the top of the stairs.

Pressing Studdington's arm to indicate caution, he felt gingerly for the first step, then drew his prisoner down beside him. In this way they went down step by step, until they reached the half-way landing.

There, as a board creaked loudly under the pressure of his foot. Tinker paused and waited; but the only sound that now broke the stillness was the slow ticking of a big grandfather clock in the hall below.

Again Tinker essayed to descend, and at last, after what seemed an eternity of time, they reached the bottom. Once more the lad waited and listened, but it seemed that all the household slept.

Now their progress was more rapid, and, being more certain of his surroundings, it did not take Tinker long to find the study door, he had already weighed the possibility of Yvonne having stayed up to work late, for he knew this was a habit of hers.

And if she should have done so on this night, then he knew she would be in the study. But he could see no line of light beneath the door, and when he had pushed it open he saw that the room was in darkness, he drew Studdington after him, and closed the door softly.

The fire still glowed a little, which made it not difficult to cross the room without colliding with a chair or a table.

At the window he paused and felt for the lock. As he thought, someone had pressed the catch into place before retiring, and Tinker emitted a faint grunt of satisfaction as he realised how wise he had been to seize his opportunity when he did. When he had pressed the catch back, he pushed up the sash until there was room to squeeze out.

As he took Studdington's arm to force him through, the latter made his first show of resistance. Something in the black, dripping night outside filled him with a dread that made him almost ready to risk a shooting, and make sufficient noise to attract Yvonne or Graves.

But the sinister pressure of the cold barrel of Tinker's pistol filled him with an even greater dread, and he surrendered. With his hands tied behind him under the big raincoat it was not easy for him to negotiate the sill, but at last Tinker managed to get him through, and dropped lightly after him.

He pulled the sash down, then, clutching his prisoner by the arm, set off through the rain, slumping through the sodden grass towards the gates.

Owing to Studdington's inability to move rapidly, it took them over half an hour to cover the distance to the village, but once free of the gates, Tinker did not mind the extra delay.

He was filled with a lively satisfaction at the result of his visit; for, even were he overtaken now and Studdington recaptured, the fact remained that he had entered the house and taken his man away under their very noses.

He knew there was going to be a problem on his arrival at the inn. In the first place, he had intimated that he would not be away more than about an hour, whereas he had been nearly three hours. Again, he would have to secure his prisoner some place where he could not be seen until he could wake the boots, pay his bill, and get the Grey Panther out.

He thought regretfully of the big bed which he had figured on occupying that night, but in view of what had happened since he left the inn, he knew that he must lose no time in getting his man as far away as possible before Yvonne should discover what had taken place.

He grinned to himself as he thought of the consternation that would reign in the morning when Studdington's disappearance was discovered. He knew that it would not take Yvonne long to pick up the trail through the unlocked window and the footprints in the soft ground outside. But that did not worry him in the least, providing he could get a start in the Grey Panther.

As he approached the village, he gazed about him in search of a suitable place to secure his prisoner. It was too dark to see anything distinctly, but just on the outskirts he remembered that there was a small clump of trees. He felt his way about until he located them, and then, after considerable stumbling over roots and other projections, he found one which he thought would serve his purpose.

Next he proceeded to remove his prisoner's coat and untie his wrists. That done, he drew his arms back until his hands met behind the tree, and in this position Tinker once more secured him. He hung the coat over him, and with a whispered threat of what he would do when he returned if the other tried to make a noise, he stole out of the grove and made for the inn.

It took him a considerable time to wake anyone, but at last he managed to rouse the boots. That individual was very sleepy and very bad-tempered, but he sulkily did Tinker's bidding when Tinker had thrust a note into his hand. He opened the small shed where the Grey Panther stood, and while Tinker examined his petrol tank, the boots got his bag. Then Tinker gave him money to pay for his food and lodging, climbed into the car.

He drove away slowly, for he did not want the boots to see whither he was bound. He kept the powerful road lamps switched off, too, and, with only the ordinary side lamps burning, drove along to the clump of trees where he had left his prisoner.

Jumping out, Tinker soon untied him, and this time secured his wrists in front. That done, he forced Studdington into the car after he had buttoned his coat about him. Then he got in himself, and, switching on the powerful road lamps, sent the Grey Panther through the village with a roar.

· · · · ·

It was just beginning to show the first faint streaks of dawn on that wet, drear autumn morning when Sexton Blake opened his eyes to find his young assistant, Tinker standing just inside the door of his room. Blake came up sitting.

"What on earth are you doing here Tinker?" he asked sharply. "Have you lost the trail?"

"I have brought Studdington back guv'nor," answered Tinker laconically. "He's in the consulting-room now."

And with an expression almost of disbelief on his countenance, Sexton Blake thrust his silk-pyjamaed legs out of bed.

Under the pressure of Blake's shoulder the door flew inwards, and as the detective staggered across the threshold he gave a sharp exclamation. Before him was the prostrate body of a man upon the floor. (*Chapter 7.*)

The Seventh Chapter. A Little Deduction —Spreading the Net —
The Call From the Yard —The Soho Tragedy —And What it
Revealed —Sir Edward is Released —Explanation —Yvonne
Receives a Lecture.

ALTHOUGH Sexton Blake was in bed and asleep when Tinker reached Baker Street to wake him with his startling announcement, that did not mean that Blake had left the fag of details to his assistant and had himself taken things easy. On the contrary. No sooner had Tinker departed for the country in the Grey Panther than Blake started on his own account.

It will be recalled that Blake considered the solving of one question of the greatest importance —that was whether Otto Bernstorm had made his accusation against Studdington before or after he knew that his wound was not dangerous.

It had been Blake's original intention to question the surgeons direct on this point, but, on second thoughts, he decided to make the inquiry through Detective Inspector Thomas of Scotland Yard.

Further, he had another request to make of the inspector. This was the outcome of both the detailed and collective analyses made by Blake during the day. He was not at all satisfied that everything was clear regarding the shooting in Bernstorm's office.

To his trained mind, there were several loose ends sticking out which no one seemed able to explain. And chief among these, in Blake's opinion, was the somewhat vague personality of the swarthy person who had called on Bernstorm shortly before the shooting, and of whom Bernstorm had made no mention.

Ordinarily, that might not loom so importantly, but, when considered in conjunction of what had followed so soon after, it raised a question in Blake's mind that could only be satisfied by the true answer.

Who was this mysterious person? Why had he refused to give his name, and yet at the same time had persisted so obstinately in seeing Bernstorm privately? Then, when Bernstorm had told his clerk that he would not see the man, why had he, when the latter had pushed his way in, so suddenly changed his decision, and had agreed to give the interview?

Following that, what length of time had elapsed from when, according to the theory generally held, Bernstorm had shown his visitor out by the door leading directly to the corridor, and the very mysterious entry of the accused man, Studdington?

Blake had dismissed, with an incredulous shrug, Bernstorm's statement that his assailant had managed to enter the office and get round in front of the desk before he heard him. Blake had not the slightest doubt that this statement was a deliberate lie, without a shred of truth in it.

His examination of the lock on the door had proved that, firstly, it was impossible to open it from the outside without the right key, or, at least, without making considerable noise in forcing it. Was it reasonable to suppose that Studdington, or anyone else, would attempt to force the lock at that hour of the day, when persons would be passing and repassing in the corridor, and, moreover, when it must be known that Bernstorm was in his room?

Blake answered the question with an emphatic negative. It was, to him, a ludicrous and senseless suggestion for a man of Bernstorm's undoubted intelligence to make. Then why had he made it?

Was it to conceal some fact which he did not wish to come out? From what he himself had said to Blake, the latter knew that the financier was mixed up in several transactions which were of such a secret nature that he was prepared to suffer the loss of the bonds which had been abstracted from his safe rather than inform the police.

Then it was not unreasonable to suppose that a similar motive might have caused him to suppress the true facts about what had happened in the office that morning.

And if this were so, then might it not be possible to go a step further, and ask if his accusation against Studdington was not also a lie? In that case, who did shoot Bernstorm?

And if it was not Studdington, then why had he accused the latter? Had he known all the time that the man he had wronged years before was out of prison? Did he fear reprisals from Studdington, and, in concealing the truth about the shooting was he also seizing the opportunity to kill two birds with one stone, so to say?

Did he plot to have Studdington sent back to prison for another long term —a term which, at his age, would mean his death behind prison walls?

Blake could not answer these questions in a definite way, but the more he thought over the matter, the more he brought that finely-attuned mind machine of his to bear on the various points, the more convinced was he that he wanted very much to find the mysterious stranger who had visited Bernstorm just before the shooting.

True, he had not much to go upon. Only a vague description, with his own theory that the man must be either an Austrian or a Hungarian—Blake inclined rather to the latter view. And, with nothing more than this as a start, he was going to give Inspector Thomas the problem of running the man to earth, hoping that the finely meshed net which the inspector would be able to out would bring the required fish into the catch, together with the inevitable collection of strays and suspects which always came to light during such a cast.

Therefore, when he had made this decision he put on his coat and hat, and walked along Baker Street until he found a taxi. He drove to Scotland Yard, where he was fortunate enough to find the inspector in his room, and, after a long, confidential conversation with that official, waited until the inspector had called up on the phone one of the surgeons who had operated on Otto Bernstorm.

The result of that conversation cleared up one point, at any rate, and cleared it in such a manner that it but served to strengthen the theory on which Blake was already working.

From the combined evidence of the surgeon and Inspector Thomas, he was able to put down as proven fact that Otto Bernstorm had made his accusation against Studdington after he knew he was in no real danger, and not before —a most significant fact to Blake's mind.

He was not able to take the inspector fully into his confidence, but he was forced to do so to a certain extent, and, when he finally left Scotland Yard on his way back to Baker Street, the lines were already humming as the great police net was being spread for the cast that evening.

There was nothing else to do then but to wait, and knowing that he would eventually hear the results of the somewhat complicated machinery he had set in motion, Blake philosophically put the affair from his mind, and dined quietly alone at Baker Street.

It is incorrect to say that he put every phase of the affair out of his mind, for, while he gave Mrs. Bardell the rare pleasure of eating the dinner she had prepared, his thoughts were on Yvonne. Although it was by no means clear to Blake just what had induced Yvonne to play a part in Sir Edward Studdington's affairs, that she did share a

73

very definite responsibility in them he was positive.

It was difficult for Blake to reconcile this with her more recent actions, for he had hoped and believed that all danger of her quixotic impulses leading her under the shadow of the law was a thing of the past.

And yet here had arisen this inexplicable occurrence in which he could scarcely attribute a minor part to Yvonne. On the contrary, the more Blake pieced the bits of the puzzle together the more positive did her association appear to be. Therefore, he was a little puzzled, a little distrait, and more than a little uneasy.

When he had finished dinner, Blake went to the laboratory, where he inspected the progress of a few experiments he was making. There was little for him to do beyond checking up temperature, and he felt too restless to settle down to anything new.

He finally drifted into the consulting-room, where he took down some of the older volumes of the famous "Index," and re-read records of the past, some of which contained more thrills and romance than any imaginings of the present day novelist. He was still in these when the telephone rang, and, lifting the receiver, he heard the voice of Inspector Thomas on the other end of the wire.

"We haven't completed the haul yet, Blake." he said: "but one of our men has reported a suspect in Soho. I can't say if it is the man you want, but he first attracted attention by his queer actions.

"He has been followed, and is at present in a small lodging-house there. Do you want to have a look at him, or will you wait until they bring the haul in?"

Blake was anxious for action of any sort, and grasped at the opportunity offered by the inspector.

"I will go along with you now, inspector," he said quickly. "Where shall we meet?"

"Well, there is just about time for a whisky-and-soda at the Venetia, so suppose we meet there?"

"Right you are! I shall go along at once." Blake hung up the receiver, and, making his way along to his dressing-room, donned a long raincoat. Then, when he had chosen a soft hat, he slipped a small automatic in his pocket. He had to walk almost to Oxford Street before he found a taxi, and when he arrived at the Venetia he found that the inspector was there already.

They went along to the bar, which was just preparing to close, and, after a whisky-and-soda, returned to the street. The inspector had dismissed his taxi, but Blake's was still waiting, so it only took a few minutes to drive along Shaftesbury Avenue, and so into Soho. The inspector rapped for the taxi to pull up at the corner of Old Compton Street, where they descended.

"We had better wait here," remarked Blake, as he got out, and, as the inspector did not object, Blake gave the necessary instructions.

They then walked along past the little restaurants which are such a feature of the district, until, at the second corner, a man came up to the inspector, and saluted.

Blake recognised him as one of the Flying Squad of the Yard.

"Everything all right?" asked the inspector curtly.

"Yes, sir. Nothing new to report. He is gone into a house kept by an Italian named Riggi. Nothing against Riggi, as far as we know, but he has some queer customers at times. Since he went in he has not come out."

"Very well. We will go along and have a talk with Riggi."

The three made their way up a side street, until the plain-clothes man came to a stop before a small house which appeared to be in absolute darkness. But to those three who knew the district so well, that meant nothing. Mounting the steps, Blake and the inspector stood aside while the Flying Squad man rapped on the door.

To their first and second summons no reply came, but at the third there was the rattle of a chain inside, and a moment later the door opened a few inches to reveal a little old man of strongly marked Latin features.

"We want a talk with you, Riggi," said the Flying Squad man curtly, as he shouldered his way into the hall.

Without a word the Italian closed the door after them, and led the way along the dingy hall to a little room at the end, which was apparently used by him as a sort of office.

There were only two chairs in the room, so his visitors made no attempt to sit down. Instead, Inspector Thomas fixed him with a stern eye, and said:

"All your rooms full at the present time?" The Italian nodded.

"Si —yes, all full."

"Got your records up to date?"

"Si —me I maka de record all right. No police maka me scared. I do nossing wrong."

"All right; let us see your book."

The old man turned obediently, and, opening a drawer in the table, took out a dirty book which was evidently his register. He opened it, and stood aside while Blake and Inspector Thomas bent over it.

The page was dirty and begrimed, and in some instances so bad was the writing that it was almost impossible to spell out the names and addresses. There had been but few arrivals in the space of a week, for over the period of seven days there were only five entries in all.

And among these five Sexton Blake suddenly picked out one to which he drew the inspector's attention.

"I'll take a chance, and say this is the man we want to interrogate," he said. "At least, I'll wager he is the man Clarke here tracked to the house."

The inspector readjusted his glasses and read: "Karl Menrich. Vienna," and under the space for nationality was written "Hungarian." It was the only name which had that part of Europe written as the domicile. The others were divided between Italy, France, and Spain.

"All right; perhaps you are right," answered the inspector. "We will have a talk to him, anyway.

"Is this man in?" he asked of Riggi, pointing out the name.

"Si —he is in not long."

"What floor?"

"De top."

"All right; take us up there. We want to have a talk with him."

As obediently as before, the old man led the way along the hall to the staircase, up which they toiled slowly. The top floor proved to be the third, and they had just started up the last flight, when all four came to a sudden stop, as a sharp report rang out from above.

The next instant, Blake, the inspector, and the Flying Squad men were dashing up the stairs, and as their eyes came on a level with the floor, they could see a thin line of light under a door which faced them. Blake was in the lead, and as he leapt across the landing his finger dropped to the handle.

A single twist told him the door was locked, so, drawing back, he sent his shoulder against it; at the same instant the inspector and Clarke hurled themselves forward. Under that pressure the door flew inwards like a piece of cardboard, and as Blake staggered in across the threshold he gave a sharp exclamation and pointed to something which lay on the floor.

The inspector and Clarke peered over his shoulder, and the inspector gave a grunt of annoyance as he realised what had happened. Before them was the body of a man huddled as he had fallen, in his right hand a heavy revolver, and in his right temple a gaping hole from which a thin trickle of blood was oozing.

"We will never talk to him now," said Blake, moving forward. "No skull ever withstood a shot like that."

And a very brief examination showed that the unknown had died instantaneously. Clarke recognised him as the man whom he had followed, and as far as Blake could see, he answered well enough to the vague description which he had been able to give to Scotland Yard.

But that did not prove that he was the man who had visited Bernstorm's office that morning. Nor did it enable them to make a definite connection between the shooting of Bernstorm and the suicide before them.

It was Blake who, in glancing about the room, suddenly saw a white envelope lying on the top of a rickety table by the bed. Snatching it up, he glanced at the address, and made out:

"Dr. Otto Menrich,
19 Balstrasse 19,
Vienna,
Austria."

"Look at this, inspector," he said, holding it out. "If you will examine the writing, you will see that the ink is scarcely dry. I think, under the circumstances, we had better open it."

"Certainly. It may throw some light on what has happened. Clarke, go along and get a constable, and ring up the divisional surgeon. Mr. Blake and I will look after things until he turns up."

Blake had already opened the letter, and was bending over the single sheet of paper it contained. He saw at a glance that it was written in the Magyar language, and apparently addressed by the dead man to his brother. He ran through it, making a free translation as he went along, and when he had finished it he nodded his head.

"You can give instructions to release the police net, inspector," he said, as he tapped the page. "We have all we want here. The man before you is the man who shot Otto Bernstorm."

"What! What do you mean, Blake?"

"Just what I say. It was because I had strong reason to doubt that the released convict Studdington did the shooting that I asked you to try and rope in this man tonight. This letter was written just before he shot himself. In it he states that it is his intention to do so. I will read it to you. It is to his brother, and runs roughly as follows:

"'My dear Brother.—It is done. I saw Bernstorm this morning, and he laughed at me. That laugh has cost him dearly. He is, I hope, by now where he will never laugh again, for I shot straight. I have fulfilled my vow, and now I go to join my dear ones. Do not hope to recover anything from Bernstorm. There is no hope. May things come right for you in time, but I fear for our unhappy country. Better had it been if we had remained in Hungary, the country of our birth. Farewell.

"Your unhappy brother,

"'KARL.'

"That is roughly what it says," remarked Blake, as he handed the letter to the inspector. "But it is sufficient evidence that this is the man who shot Bernstorm."

"But I don't understand this at all, Blake. Bernstorm accuses Studdington of the shooting. He states most positively that the man who tried to kill him was like Studdington, only he thought Studdington was still in prison."

Blake's lips curled.

"In making that statement Bernstorm lied," he said. "I hope before long to prove to you that Bernstorm was perfectly aware that Studdington had been released from prison, and that he also knew that it was this man who shot him."

"But what could be his reasons for making such a statement?" exclaimed the puzzled inspector.

"I have strong hopes that we shall force that reason from Bernstorm's own lips," responded Blake. "I hope to have completed my inquiries by to-morrow, and, in any event, this matter must be cleared up without delay. Will you act on this letter, and call off the hue-and-cry after Studdington? If you wish to interrogate him, I expect to be able to produce him."

Inspector Thomas cocked an eye at Blake. "Do you know where he is?"

"To be perfectly frank, I think I do."

"Well, you produce him, and I will have a talk with him. I want to hear what he has to say about this. In the meantime, I will call off the hunt."

And it was with this arranged that Sexton Blake was forced to be content. His greatest worry was that Tinker might fail to get hold of Studdington in time, and that, in order to keep his word to the inspector, he would be forced to take such measures that Yvonne's participation must become known.

But he put that from him for the time being, and until long into the night worked with the inspector and the surgeon over the case which had claimed their attention in such a dramatic manner.

It was nearly morning when they had completed their work, and had taken measures to despatch the body to the proper place. They parted at Piccadilly Circus, and the last words the inspector uttered were words of admonition to Blake. Considering all this, it can well be imagined what Blake's feelings were when he was woke by Tinker at dawn with the laconic announcement that he had his man waiting in the consulting-room.

As soon as they had got well started on the road Tinker had removed the gag from between his prisoner's teeth, but he had kept his wrists tied together; and although Studdington had made several attempts to get some information out of his youthful captor, Tinker had maintained a steady silence the whole way.

As a matter of fact, from the first moment of his discovery of Tinker's youth, Studdington had lost a good deal of the fear he had felt when he had first been faced by the fiendish-looking mask that Tinker had donned for his purpose.

And while he felt a little foolish at having allowed himself to be captured by one so young, and, moreover, by one whose features certainly did not seem to back up the vicious threats Tinker had uttered, he still found that his abductor was extremely cool and efficient.

Therefore, it was with a feeling of trepidation still gripping him that he watched anxiously for the door of the consulting-room to reopen, he had no idea, so far, that he was in Sexton Blake's house.

Nor did he know that the tall man who came in, clad in a silk dressing-gown, was the famous detective. But he had little time to wonder about his identity in the amazement which filled him at the other's actions.

Instead of surveying him as one would a prisoner, Blake crossed the room with a smile, and in a few deft twists had loosened the cord with which Tinker had bound Studdington's wrists. Then he made an apology for the manner in which he had been treated.

"I trust we shall be able to make up for it," he said. "I am Sexton Blake. It was necessary that I should have you here without delay, so I gave the instructions to my assistant. It was the only way, for I knew that if I took any other your —er—hostess would probably refuse to give you up.

"I will enlighten you on one point, and then we shall see about some tea, after which we can discuss matters. The one point to which I refer is the shooting of Otto Bernstorm."

"Mr. Blake, I swear to you that I know nothing of that!"

"I am already aware of that, Sir Edward," responded Blake, with a smile. "Last night I ran down the man who did the shooting. Unfortunately, he committed suicide before we could reach him; but he left behind a letter which contained a confession. And it is that confession which clears you."

Studdington sank back in the chair with a gasp of relief.

"But the taking of certain bonds from Otto Bernstorm's safe is another matter," went on Blake coolly. "That is what we shall discuss later. For that discussion I shall require the presence of your late hostess. In the meantime, we shall have tea."

Forthwith Blake sent Tinker, who was as amazed as Studdington at his words, to rouse Mrs. Bardell.

•　　•　　•　　•　　•

It was just a few minutes before nine o'clock when Mademoiselle Yvonne stepped out of her big touring car in front of her flat at Queen Anne's Gate, telling Alec to wait. The day before it had been her intention to return to town just as early as possible in order to watch developments there, and thus it was that she had started out at dawn without the faintest idea that her guest had been kidnapped overnight.

Therefore, she was hardly prepared to find Anna, her maid, in a state of extreme agitation when she entered the flat. It took her only a few minutes to get the story. When Studdington had not come down, Graves had gone to his room, thinking he had overslept. It was then he had made the discovery, and had been on the telephone asking if Yvonne had reached the flat. With curt orders to the maid to put through a trunk-call immediately, Yvonne picked up the letters that had come by the morning post.

On the very top of the pile was one unstamped, and Yvonne had no difficulty in recognising the writing on the envelope.

Tearing it open, she took out the folded sheet, and no sooner had she cast her eyes down the page than she called sharply to Anna to cancel the trunk-call. For although the letter was short, it was sufficient to tell Yvonne that the game had been taken out of her hands —snapped up while she had slept —and that by the very man at whom she had mocked the previous day. It ran thus:

Mademoiselle, —I hope that this will reach you as soon as you arrive from Hampshire. I am sorry that it has been necessary to remove your guest so unceremoniously, but I found it necessary to question him on one or two matters, and the course I took was the only one possible. We are now in conference at Baker Street, and I shall be glad if you will come round as soon as possible after your arrival. There are certain points to be cleared up before I see Inspector Thomas, and you are the only person who can clear them up. — Yours,

  "SEXTON BLAKE."

Anna gazed in bewilderment as Yvonne turned and flew out of the room.

And not many minutes later Yvonne was standing in the consulting-room at Baker Street under the cool and somewhat amused scrutiny of Sexton Blake.

 • • • • •

Half an hour later Sexton Blake swung back in his chair.

"Well, I guess we have dealt with everything," he said. "I will go on at once and see Otto Bernstorm; then I will drive to Scotland Yard, and have a talk with Inspector Thomas. It will be necessary for you to stand by Sir Edward, for the inspector will want to interrogate you. After that I will stop at your offices, Mademoiselle Yvonne and let you hear the result.

"Now, while it is not for me to discuss the ethics of this affair, I sincerely trust you will not run your necks into such a noose again. I sympathise fully with sir Edward, and I am prepared to believe that a grave injustice was done him.

"At the same time, the general results of the methods of our British law are sound and just, and if everybody allocated to himself the right to take his own vengeance, then we should have nothing but chaos."

And on completing his little lecture, Blake became once more the genial host.

Exactly what passed during the private interview that Blake had with Otto Bernstorm no one would ever know.

The nearest Tinker ever got to guessing what might have transpired —and that was nearer than anyone else would ever get — was the few muttered words which Blake let fall as he entered the car:

"Thorough bounder —if —wasn't wounded wouldn't have let — off so easily!"

From Upper Brook Street they drove to Scotland Yard, where Blake fulfilled his promise to Inspector Thomas and when that was over, Tinker turned the car towards Oxford Street. Blake left the lad in the car and made his way slowly up the stairs.

Yvonne watched him as his broad shoulders disappeared behind the closing door, and her eyes became very tender.

"You are a wonderful criminologist, Mr. Blake," she said softly, "but there are a few things yet you might learn about my sex."

And whatever she might have meant by those enigmatic words. Mademoiselle Yvonne kept securely locked in her own shapely head.

THE END.
[30200 WORDS]

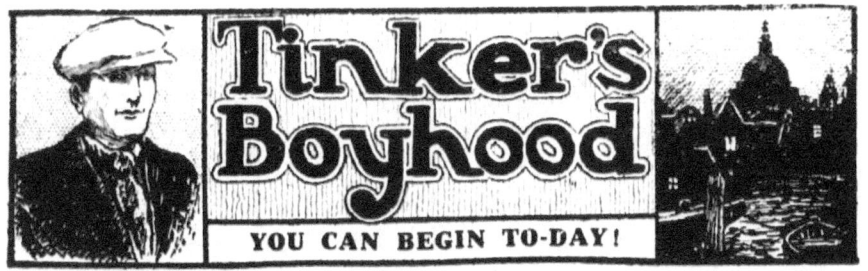

Tinker's Boyhood

This Splendid Yarn is a record, grave and gay, of the adventures of the lad who afterwards became the youthful friend and confidant of Sexton Blake. The story of his boyhood will delight you as much as do those of his later fame. Please mention this tale to your friends.

The First Chapters...

Tinker, in the days before he met Sexton Blake, comes into contact with a master criminal known as the Baron, whose plans, with the aid of a mysterious stranger —Mr. Allandale, or Nemo —he succeeds in thwarting. He eventually falls into the Baron's hands, and is sentenced to death, a man known as the Doctor being detailed for this work. But the Doctor, Tinker later learns, is his friend, Mr. Allandale.

The Baron is tricked into believing his orders have been carried out, and Tinker is sent to join a country paper and lie low. But there he learns of an intended bank robbery, and returns to tell Mr. Allandale, who whistles with surprise.

(Now read on.)

An Experiment.

"I'd no idea he was back in England. I heard he was still in hiding in Paris. Things must be getting pretty critical for him to venture back."

"He's back, right enough, sir, but he's disguised," said Tinker. "He's got a black beard, and looks altogether different. But I knew his eyes at once, and I just had to come."

Mr. Allandale nodded, and stared at the carpet, lost in thought.

"A bank robbery!" he said at last. "Where?"

"At Marlington, where I was —a place called Berriton's Bank. They expect to get twenty thousand pounds to-morrow night."

The exclamation sounded as though Tinker's explanation had cleared up some puzzling point, and Mr. Allandale retired into his own thoughts again, whilst Tinker sat and watched.

"It's worth trying," said Allandale, half to himself, at length. "It may fail, but I don't think it will; and if it does —well, we shall see!"

He rose abruptly, fumbled in his pockets, and produced a small case which he laid on the table; then he stepped quickly to the window, pulled the edge of the curtain back a fraction of an inch, and peered out.

He seemed to look more at the sky than at the street below, gave a nod of satisfaction, and came swiftly back to the table.

"Take your collar off," he ordered, "and rumple your hair! That's it! Now, then, off with your coat and waistcoat, and sit down there whilst I get to work! Quick! There's no time to be lost!"

Tinker obeyed, and Mr. Allandale opened his case. It contained merely a few sticks of ordinary grease-paint, and some odds-and-ends of make-up.

"We're going to try the Baron's nerves," he said; "and they're pretty bad just now. I'll tell you about all that afterwards."

With deft touches he rubbed some of the grease-paint over Tinker's face, put in a few lines here and there with his finger-tips, scooped a handful of water from the jug on the washhand-stand, and soused Tinker's hair till it hung limp and dank, and the drops trickled down his face, and stood back a couple of paces to survey his handiwork just as an artist steps back from a canvas.

"You'll do!" he said. "Look at yourself in the glass! It's only an experiment, but I think it will work!"

He pushed Tinker towards the glass, and held the candle above his head so that he could see better.

Tinker looked at his own reflection, and gave a stifled cry. He was unprepared, and had not known what to expect, and the result gave him a shock.

His face was a ghastly, greenish white, with the water-soaked hair lying dank on his forehead, which gleamed with drips of moisture. There were deep purplish shadows under his eyes which made them look hollow and sunken, and a gruesome splash of something reddish on his throat, just where long ago Allandale had scratched his skin with a knife in the deserted barn, and where a faint scar still remained. Beneath that his shirt gleamed dully white, and was open at the neck.

"Pretty grim —eh?" said Mr. Allandale.

"It's— it's beastly!" gulped Tinker.

"So is the brute yonder in my rooms waiting for me!" said Mr. Allandale, and blew out the candle.

"Now come, and do exactly as I tell you."

He pressed the spring of the near mirror, and they stepped into the dark passage once more.

Mr. Allandale led the way, moving with extreme care, and having reached the end of the passage, peered into the far room.

"Stand here," he whispered; and, taking Tinker by the shoulders, placed him carefully in position. "Now keep your eyes closed, and, whatever happens, don't move. You won't be hurt —I'll see to that. Even if he looses off that revolver he was fiddling with just now, you're not to stir. You understand?"

"Yes," said Tinker.

"Get ready, then!"

Tinker heard him fumbling softly in the darkness, and a sound as of a tap being gently turned.

The little beam of light coming through the peephole in the mirror from the room beyond diminished in brightness and flickered out.

Tinker heard a hoarse exclamation, and felt a sudden draught of wind on his face, by which he knew that Mr. Allandale had pressed the spring, and that the mirror had swung back noiselessly, leaving an open space.

From where he stood he knew that the lower edge of the opening must be just about on a level with his chest, and from beneath his eyelids he was aware of a faint flicker of moonlight filtering through the unshuttered windows opposite on to his face slantwise.

There was a choking sound, a harsh, stifled scream, and then a blaze of red light and a blare of noise —the crash of a heavy revolver fired in a confined space.

Three times the Baron fired. There was a reek of burnt powder; a few grains stung Tinker's cheeks, but that was all. And then there came a crash of a different kind —the thud of a heavy falling body, and of a chair being overturned. Again there came a gentle stirring of cool wind as the mirror clicked back into its place, and the lights were turned on once more.

"Look!" whispered Allandale in his ear.

Tinker looked, and saw the Baron lying face downwards on the floor, his arms asprawl, and the still smoking revolver clutched in his right hand.

"Fainted," said Allandale tersely, "or in a fit of some kind. Anyway, he's had a scare that will last him a lifetime. Listen! He's roused the house!"

(Another thrilling instalment next week. Order your copy now.)

No. 22.   Presented with the UNION JACK Library for the week ending September 30th, 1922.

"BALMIES."

By T. C. BRIDGES.

"Balmy" is prison slang for a man who is not quite right in his head; but it is also used to mean all persons who are eccentric in any way. Some of the more interesting cases of this type which have appeared in British prisons from time to time are described in the following article.

"Balmies."

By T. C. Bridges.

"Balmy" is prison slang for a man who is not quite right in his head; but at is also used to mean all persons who are eccentric in any way. Some of the more interesting cases of this type which have appeared in British prisons from time to time are described in the following article.

LIKE the outside world, prisons often contain specimens of humanity who are different mentally from their follows. They are known as "balmies."

A convict who is really of weak intellect is usually sent to Parkhurst, where he is given a very easy time; but in all prisons you will find certain characters who are sound enough to do their work all right, yet are a little odd in one way or another.

I remember one such at Dartmoor.

A little man, not more than five feet high. He was a good worker, and in most respects what is called a "good prisoner." Now the prison parties at Dartmoor walk two and two when going to or coming from their tasks.

When I first saw the man I was standing with a prison official in the yard, watching the farm parties coming in from work, and as one party passed I noticed this little man walking quite by himself behind the rest.

Naturally, I made inquiries.

The official laughed.

"He does it because he won't walk with the other. We spent months trying to make him do so. He was punished over and over again, but he stuck to his guns, and at last he fairly beat us. He works well, gives no trouble in other respects, so in the end we have allowed him to have his way."

Another man in Dartmoor made a curious request of the governor. He asked for a cell on the top floor of No. 5 Prison. The average convict hates being perched up at the top of this very lofty prison, for to them it seems an aggravation of loneliness.

Naturally, the governor inquired the man's reason for this odd request.

"Well, you see, sir. I don't like to have no one over my head." was his rather vague answer. His request was granted; but later the governor, visiting him in his cell, got the man to talk confidentially.

He explained that he was an old sailor, that he did not care about reading, for it made his head ache, and that he liked to walk up and down his cell, listening to the wind howling overhead, which made him think that he was at sea again.

Another convict, sentenced to twenty years for manslaughter, passionately asserted at his trial that the homicide was justifiable, and that the judge was committing a crime in passing such a sentence. He swore that it should not be carried out.

When he had finished his "separates," and was brought to Dartmoor, he flatly refused to do the usual work. He would clean his cell, he would even march out to labour with his party, but nothing would induce him to handle pick or shovel.

The prisoner would lie on his bed as though dead, making it necessary for two warders to dress and undress him.

He was sent to the punishment cells, his diet was reduced to bread and water, and he was, of course, docked of stage and remission, and all the other privileges, such as letters and visits and library books.

Yet nothing altered his iron determination, and he continued to refuse to do a hand's turn for the public. This, although he knew that it would add five long years to his sentence.

In the end he was left alone, and spent the long, dreary days by himself, in his cell. He was a tall, grey, silent man, and before his long sentence was completed his hair was white as snow.

A Remarkable Convict.

The well-known "Dartmoor Shepherd" was another curious example of a man who was crooked in only one way. When let out he would always break into a church. Goodness knows why, for very often he got very little for his pains except a new sentence.

When in prison his conduct was excellent, and his skill with sheep amazing. He never walked behind his sheep, as is the usual custom with English shepherds.

The sheep followed him in Eastern fashion, and sometimes, when a lamb broke away and refused to be driven by the dogs, he would go back and call it by name, when it would at once follow him.

The Dartmoor shepherd was a convict whose skill with sheep was amazing. They followed him instead of him following them.

This old man disliked nothing worse than being discharged from prison. You see, by the end of one of his long sentences he had gained, by good conduct, all the privileges possible, but when he came back as he always did within three months —all these were forfeited, and he had to work up again from the beginning.

There are always a number of old lags of his type in any convict prison, men whose conduct in prison is perfect, but who simply cannot run straight outside.

I have known a man of his type actually burst into tears when saying good bye to the governor, and it is not uncommon for a prisoner to beg that he may be kept on in prison, saying that it is the only home he has ever known.

Offended Dignity.

One of these poor old men, who had served many sentences in Dartmoor, had eventually got the job of prison whitewash man. His special care was the prison lavatories. Discharged, he tried to keep honest, but in the end fell on evil days and was taken to the workhouse. From there he wrote to the governor of Dartmoor, complaining bitterly of his position. "I didn't think, sir," he wrote, "as the governor would let their sanitary inspector come as low as this."

But all "balmies" are not so amiable as those I have been describing. You get a type of man with an uncontrollable temper who is the bane of warders and convicts alike.

A famous case was that of "Miss" Julia Newman. She was a West Indian, of good birth, an artist and musician, but a "crook" from the word "Go!"

Eventually she found her way into Millbank Prison, where she soon proved herself a holy terror. She had the temper of a wild cat, and was possessed of the strength of a tigress.

The wardresses were terrified of her, and even when they had succeeded in subduing her, and tying her up, she would break free and go for them like a mad thing. For the whole year of her imprisonment she kept the prison in a state of siege, and the officials were only too thankful when the time for her release at last arrived.

You get men of similar type, and their fate is usually a "bashing." Horrible as flogging may seem, it is the only cure for a brute of this sort, and I have known several cases of old lags whose conduct was simply perfect, but who bore upon their backs marks of the lash inflicted perhaps twenty years previously.

Cock of the Walk

The type of bully sometimes seen in the public school or Army is not unknown in prison. Some years ago there was a man of this type in a quarry party at Dartmoor. He was a big man, and soon made himself cock of the walk. He made the lives of his companions a misery, and no one dared say a word to him.

One day there was a new recruit in the party, a middle sized man not very young. In fact, his hair was beginning to grizzle. He was in for manslaughter.

The bully was not long in getting to work upon him, and for a time the new man took it quietly enough. But presently, in moving a stone, he turned it over so sharply that the bully got his toes pinched. He turned on the other viciously, with a torrent of low-voiced, but none the less bitter, abuse.

The new man looked up at him.

"Chuck that!' he remarked quietly.

"Chuck it? 'Oo are you talking to? I'll bash the face off ye!" And, with that, he struck him.

In a flash the newcomer had straightened up, and the two were at it hammer and tongs.

Bullying Didn't Pay.

Now, in matters like these warders exercise a wide discretion.

Although fighting is, of course, strictly forbidden, yet when two prisoners meet with fists only, they are generally allowed to fight a round or so. A little of this kind of thing may save much more serious trouble later on.

In this particular case, too, the warders were only too pleased to see anyone with pluck enough to stand up to the bully.

The bully swept a shower of blows at his smaller opponent, but the latter evaded them with curious ease. Furious, the bully drew back, then dashed in again, hitting harder than ever.

What happened next was so quick that the eager eyes of the watchers could hardly follow it. There was the thud of one well planted blow, and the bully flung up his arms and crashed to the quarry floor. There he lay, dazed and stunned, until a warder sent one of the party for a bucket of water, which was thrown over him.

Later, the two were taken before the prison governor, who had of course already heard the story. To the victor he merely said: "This is your first offence. I shall not punish you, but do not let it occur again."

To the other, both of whose eyes were in mourning, he remarked: "You seem to have had your punishment already. You can go to your cell."

The bully had indeed had his punishment, and never again did he attempt any of his old tricks. He was not likely to, for presently it was whispered that the quiet, elderly man was really J. H., who, in his youth, had been a boxer of high repute.

One of the most troublesome prisoners of recent years was the man known as Stinie Morrison, but whose real name was Morristein.

This man, a foreigner, was sentenced to death for the murder of Leon Beron on Clapham Common, but the Home Secretary reprieved him, and he was given penal servitude for life.

Making Trouble.

He served his "separates" in Wandsworth Prison, and was taken from there to Dartmoor.

On the way down he was very disorderly, shouting, and giving the warders much trouble, so when he arrived he was taken before the governor, and given as punishment fourteen days No. 2 diet. This is principally porridge and potatoes and bread.

Then he was ordered to have his hair cut. He refused, and made fresh trouble, but the job was soon done. That night he refused to take off his clothes, and when a warder went to his cell he caught hold of him and struck him a heavy blow.

Another warder went to the rescue, and Morrison's clothes were forcibly removed.

The doctor was fetched, but Morrison insolently refused to answer any questions. Two warders were placed on night duty in the man's cell, for it was feared he would attempt to commit suicide.

During the whole of his stay in prison the man was constantly giving trouble. Eventually he became ill, and died.

Foreign prisoners often give much trouble to the authorities.

One of the strangest cases on record was that of Schreiner, a German butler accused of murdering his employer and the latter's wife and mother in Cardiganshire.

When first imprisoned, the man made an effort to starve himself to death, but this was prevented by forcible feeding. After that he would refuse to eat for one or two days on end, then jump up, and, with brute-like voracity, devour the food left in his cell.

"Swinging the Lead."

Then he would lie down upon the floor and remain as still as if dead. For a day or more at a time he would stare into space, motionless and speechless. It would be necessary to dress and undress him as though he were a doll.

The question was whether he was really mad or the most wonderful "malingerer" on record. All the usual tests were applied, but it was not for a long time that it was decided that he was simply shamming.

"Malingering," as it is called, is a line of conduct that the prison doctor is always up against. The lazy lag will do anything to "fetch the farm," otherwise, to gain the infirmary, where he can lie in bed and do no work.

I remember one man who had bruised his leg, and got a nasty sore. He was put to bed, but do what he would, the doctor could not get that sore to heal. In fact, it got so bad that the man was in danger of losing his leg.

At last an orderly caught the man in the act of removing from the wound a piece of brass wire which he had hidden in his mattress, and with which he irritated the wound at night.

The prisoner's hands were then fastened up by night, and in a week or two he was well again and sent out to work.

I have usually confined my articles to those relating to prisoners in British prisons, but I must mention a curious case which I heard of in the States.

A man named Patrick Hanley was confined in the Massachusetts State Prison for making counterfeit money. His sentence was ten years. When he was sentenced he vowed that he would not speak a word during his whole term of imprisonment, and, incredible as it seems, he kept his oath.

When at last his sentence was up he found his mother and sister waiting for him outside.

Nemesis!

He smiled at them, and apparently tried to speak. But he could not. Hanley was dumb in earnest. Long disuse had paralysed the muscles of speech, and it was many days before he was able to enunciate a single word.

It was the Suffragettes who originated the hunger strike which has given so much trouble to prison authorities.

Some few years ago a man called Davis was sentenced at Biggleswade to fifteen months hard labour for theft. He was a most refractory prisoner, and presently started hunger striking.

He would drink a little milk, but flatly refused to eat. Nor would he do any work or take any exercise. It was necessary to get two warders to lead him round the exercise yard.

Yet the man was quite sane. His conduct was simply the result of reading the papers and resolving to imitate Suffragette tactics. In the end, in spite of everything the doctors could do for him, the unfortunate man died.

I have mentioned that, when there is bad blood between two convicts, the warders wisely allow a little fighting to relieve the tension. When there is no such means of evening matters up, the result may be a tragedy, such as occurred in Knutsford Gaol.

A prisoner named Tighe had a grudge against another named Halsall. Tighe found a piece of iron; he sharpened it, and made it into a sort of dagger, and succeeded in hiding it so that even the warders failed to find it.

Then he waited his chance. It came one day, when he found Halsall exactly in front of him in the prison chapel. The service was proceeding, when suddenly Tighe leaned forward and plunged his knife into Halsall's back.

Sent to Coventry.

Warders sprang to the victim's aid, and were only just in time to prevent Tighe stabbing the other a second time.

This man Tighe was quite a youngster, and was in prison on a charge of assaulting the governor of Walton Gaol.

In a previous article I told of the queer social distinctions in prison, and of how at Camp Hill the aristocracy demanded separate tables, and refused to mix with the smaller fry of crime. More reasonable was the curious boycott enacted at Pentbridge.

A man was brought into this prison who had served a previous term there, and whose conduct during that term had been such that no one —not even the vilest —would associate with him.

This time the inmates resolved that they would not put up with him at all, and a secret Union was formed to put the fellow "in Coventry." The governor set him to work in a "shop," but the moment he entered all the others dropped their tools, and refused to do a stroke so long as he was in the building.

The man was taken to another shop, with exactly similar consequences.

An official inquiry was held, at which a spokesman put forward by the convict union stated the case. In the end a slight punishment was inflicted upon the ringleaders of the "union." but the "undesirable" was transferred to another prison.

One more story, this to show that prison life is not without its humorous side.

Two men, whom we will call A and B, were sent to prison for

short terms, and were both confined in Wandsworth Gaol. A's time was up on Tuesday and B's on Wednesday. The two men exchanged identification cards, with the result that B was released on Tuesday and went away in A's clothes.

When A's turn came to be released he raised a nice outcry. His clothes were gone, and B's, he vowed, were mere rags. He refused to wear them.

To get over the difficulty and save bother, the warders subscribed and purchased for A a brand-new suit.

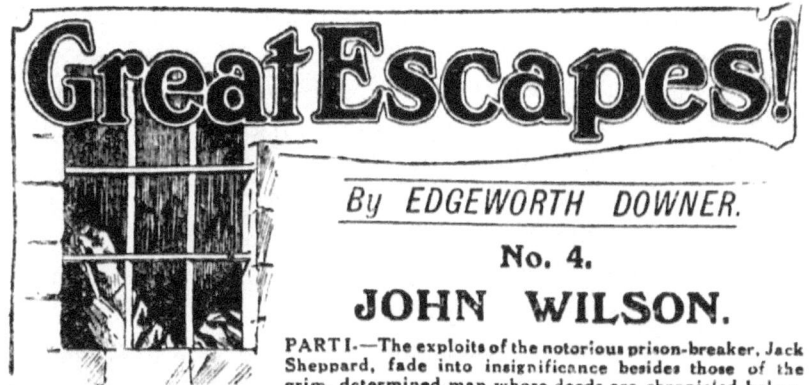

By EDGEWORTH DOWNER.

No. 4.

JOHN WILSON.

PART I.—The exploits of the notorious prison-breaker, Jack Sheppard, fade into insignificance besides those of the grim, determined man whose deeds are chronicled below.

Great Escapes!
By Edgeworth Downer.
No. 4.
JOHN WILSON.

PART I- The exploits of the notorious prison-breaker, Jack Sheppard, fade into insignificance besides those of the grim, determined man whose deeds are chronicled below.

A LITTLE more than fifteen years ago an obscure prisoner, known on the records as John Wilson, got away by some mysterious route and method from the State prison of North Carolina, at Raleigh.

The officials of the prison could not for a long time come to any conclusions about the escape of this man. He had been very ill in the hospital, and the day guard of that ward had seen him there a few minutes before he went off duty.

But when the night guard reached the hospital a few minutes later there was no such man in the room. He had vanished.

How, when, by what means, no one knew. Nor did the officials of the penal house know anything precise about this young convict.

He had been sent up less than a year before for bank robbery, and he had been sentenced to serve sixteen and one-half years.

Whence he came, what manner of criminal he was, where he might be hunted —all this was unknown.

Neither did anyone dream that this presumably commonplace felon had made a prison-break that stands and will stand with the greatest escapes of all time.

He had managed such a feat as men imagine and remember, and eventually make into history.

Gaolbreakers.

To clarify the reader's understanding of this man's deed and the qualities that make it extraordinary, it is necessary to consider for a moment what constitutes greatness in a prison break. Dr. Guede, the recognised French student of this curious subject, makes the observation that most of the famous escapes of history were managed only through assistance from outside the prison.

In some cases, says this scholar, this aid has amounted to opening the gates of the walled city by means of bribery, and he hints that this was true in the case of Casanova, whose story of his escape from the Piombi at Venice has thrilled generations of readers.

It was certainly the case in the escape of Eddie Guerin from the French penal colony in Guiana, probably the most celebrated event of the kind in American criminal annals.

Quality of Escapes.

Dr. Guede makes the patent observation that there is no greatness and no quality to escape managed in this fashion, and he goes on to remark that a prisoner who has received any sort of aid from other men, either inside or outside the prison, can hardly be considered in the eleat company of gaol-breakers.

Only the man who plays the lone hand and conquers apparently insuperable obstacles by means of his single strength, patience, and resource, can rank with the first file of prison heroes.

If, as sometimes happens, special precautions have been taken against some particular prisoner, and extra detentions thrown about him, and yet he manages to free himself, his deed becomes exalted still further.

And that was the fact in the case of John Wilson, who might as well have been called John Doe or Richard Doe, for all the clue his prison name gave to the identity of the man.

A Band of "Yeggs."

Two years before John Wilson made his memorable escape from Raleigh, several gangs of professional bank robbers invaded the south-eastern States and played havoc with the obsolete safes of the financial houses in that part of the country.

The vaults of bankers popped open like over-heated cans with disconcerting regularity for month after month, and cash amounts ranging from a few thousand to upwards of a hundred thousand dollars fell to the burglars in single hauls.

The whole of the south-east was excited, and half the towns slept beside arms to repel these unwelcome adventurers.

One of these gangs had for its junior member this man John Wilson, whose true name will not be used by this writer, for the reason that the man has long since reformed and become a successful and respectable man of business.

He was then twenty-two years of age, and had been associated with safe and bank-robbing gangs since his fifteenth year, when he had run away from home and had been picked up and initiated by a gang of inferior robbers.

Wilson had participated in a number of successful bank robberies in North and South Carolina and West Virginia at the time of his arrest for the robbery of a bank at Latta, North Carolina, but he had taken no part in the crime for which he was indicted and tried, together with two other men who were not bank robbers at all, but tramp workmen, such as the underworld calls "finks" or "shovel stiffs."

A Wrong Conviction.

Nevertheless, all three of these men were convicted of the Latta crime.

As the powerful corrosive ate into his flesh Wilson staggered to the door of the prison kitchen, where he collapsed.

Feeling was running away with judicial care. The jury apparently decided that, if Wilson and his two companions to the trouble had not committed the Latta job, they certainly had been guilty of other crimes as bad. In Wilson's case this was true enough, yet one can hardly blame the man if he felt injured and falsely condemned. He entered the prison with the resolve to escape.

This determination was strengthened and kept alive by the prison conditions then extent in many southern penal houses.

The work imposed upon the convicts was impossibly heavy and arduous, so that all but the strongest broke under it. The food was coarse, and meagre to the last extreme, and the discipline of a sort that has now happily been modified nearly everywhere.

Extreme physical punishments were, perhaps, the least objectionable feature of this notion of prison government.

This is not intended as an accusation against any single prison or any prison officials personally. It was merely the application of the old order of penology, the conception that men were put to prison not to be reformed, or treated, or corrected, but to be punished and cowed, and perhaps flogged into repentance.

The world is finding out by degrees that this scheme doesn't work.

Chances of Escape.

John Wilson had not been in prison twenty-four hours before he began to study the whole institution, seeking its weak spot. A daylight escape was impossible, he concluded, after some weeks, for the guard towers at the corners of the enclosure and along the stockade were mounted from dawn till dark by armed keepers, who kept exceptionally alert watch over the men inside the walls.

He found, too, that the cells were so arranged and so constructed as to put beyond the range of possibility any scheme for cutting out by night. He attempted to communicate with his confederates on the outside, but they were themselves either in gaol or under sharp surveillance and could give him no aid.

So he had to manage his delivery alone, and he could do it neither by day from the prison yard nor by night from his cell. Apparently he was doomed to stay in prison for sixteen and one-half years, and a less determined man must have accepted this lot, but Wilson understood that there is a point of weakness in any human structure, and that the man who seeks long enough will discover it.

After he had been inside three or four months, still watching ceaselessly for the slip or oversight that might open the way to freedom, Wilson was slightly injured in a machine-shop accident, and sent to the hospital to have his wound dressed.

He was there less than half an hour, but in that time he managed to examine his surroundings and to conclude that escape from the hospital was not beyond the range of the possible.

A Plan of Campaign.

Soon afterward he made a feigned toothache the pretext for going to the hospital again, in order that he might look a little more closely at the equipment and structure of the place.

While he waited to have his tooth looked after, he made an excuse to go to the hospital bath-room and lavatory. To his great delight, he saw here a small window, although heavily barred with steel, opening directly into the sunlight.

If he could cut these bars and knot a few sheets together he might gain the prison yard, five floors below him. If this were done quietly in the watches of some dark night it might well open the way to freedom.

John Wilson found, or believed he had found, the fatal flaw.

How to procure a tool for attacking the window bars was his next problem. He could hope for nothing from outside. Not only were his comrade, of other days too concerned with their own safety to aid him in any way, but he was himself the object of special attention and watching in the prison.

A Dangerous Prisoner.

Though he was hardly more than a boy, and though the prison knew nothing of his past save that he had been convicted as a bank robber, he was considered a dangerous prisoner, and no chances were taken.

Obviously Wilson had to get what tools he could within his prison house. To this end he finally got himself shifted to the machine shop, and there he came upon a file sufficiently good to use against one-inch steel bars.

But to procure and retain possession of this file was another matter. Such tools were dealt out to prison workmen with great care, and at the end of every working day they were as carefully collected.

The men who ran this prison understood that safety lay in sedulous attention to these details. Wilson got hold of the desired file on various occasions when he seemed to need it in his shop work, but, do what he might, he could not retain possession of this precious weapon of freedom.

He had to settle down and play a waiting game with the keeper who had charge of the tools. Sooner or later, he knew, this man would grow a little careless, or commit some oversight, or let himself be tricked in one way or another.

A Clever Ruse.

Finally, after two months of waiting and watching, Wilson caught the keeper off guard one morning, called his attention to a little blaze of shavings in the far end of the shop, and got the officer to desert the open toolbox.

In a twinkling that precious file was hid in the convict's blouse, whence it vanished to find a hiding-place in the sole of his shoe.

Wilson had now to contrive to get into the hospital and stay there for a week or two. To simulate an illness was out of the question, for he was a healthy, strong young man, and the prison physician was any thing but lenient.

He was, in fact, an old Army doctor, and he had no patience with slight ills and petty ailments. Wilson must find a way to injure himself, or make himself so ill that there would be no question about his retention in the hospital.

After many unsuccessful attempts, he managed to get himself transferred from the machine shop to the kitchen of the prison, where he was put to scrubbing floors.

In this way he got hold of a can of lye and a bar of yellow laundry soap.

Wilson took himself off into a corner, wetted his left forearm from wrist to elbow, and shook on the powdered lye.

Desperate Measures.

What tortures he must have suffered while this powerful corrosive ate into his flesh, the reader can best imagine for himself.

He had the self-command and courage to hold on and let himself be deeply burned. But this was not enough. To make himself ill and helpless beyond question he devoured part of the cake of soap, in addition to the agony of his burning arm.

Presently a dreadful nausea seized him, and he turned and ran towards the kitchen door, and collapsed as he reached it, foaming at the mouth and tearing with his teeth at his tortured arm.

He was carried to the hospital and put to bed. There could be no question of his staying there, for his arm was horribly burned, and the soap not only made him ill, but had caused an inflammation of the alimentary tract, that might have resulted fatally to a less rugged man.

He lay there, anguished by burns and high fever, but he was a happy sufferer, for he knew that in the sole of one of his shoes, poked under his bed, lay the instrument of liberation. He could hardly contain himself while he waited for the return of sufficient strength to make work possible.

The Lay of the Land.

In those days the hospital wards of the Raleigh Prison were two large rooms on the top floor of the factory building. On the left of the hall which bisected this floor was the room for negroes, and on the right that for whites.

One keeper attended both rooms, assisted, when occasion demanded, by convict nurses, and at certain hours of the day by the prison physician.

The doors giving ingress to these two rooms from the hall were nearly opposite, and each was closed by a strong steel grille, which the keeper locked after him on entering and leaving either room.

Wilson saw, as soon as he began to convalesce, that he would have to work at the bars of the bath-room window in short snatches, as often as the guard was out of the room and he could make some pretext for retiring to the lavatory.

He must cut a few strokes, and then leave off, hiding his cutting by smearing the bar with a little dust and dirt, and carefully brushing away the filings.

The danger of discovery was great, but it was somewhat reduced by the fact that there were at the time only three other men in the white hospital ward, and by a certain somnolence of the night keeper.

Choosing a Partner.

The greatest danger lay, however, in the possibility that he might recover too rapidly and be sent out of the hospital to his cell before he could get the bars cut through.

In order to speed up cutting, Wilson resolved to take one of the other convicts into his confidence, and offer the man liberty in return for his aid. He studied the other three men, and finally selected the one he deemed most trustworthy and resolute.

This man was approached after some sounding, and he readily

agreed to enter the plot. Now there were two men sneaking off to the lavatory as often as they dared and taking a few furtive swipes at the steel bar.

Finally, in the early hours of a thrilling morning, Wilson took the final cuts at the second bar, and filled up his cutting with dirt and soap to hide the wound in the steel. Both bars now hung by a mere thread. A quick jerk would take them out of the way whenever the plotters wished.

Both Wilson and his confederate decided to wait for a stormy night, when there might be noise enough from the wind and thunder to conceal their movements from the slumbering keeper.

They waited and suffered.

Would it never storm? Would Wilson recover and be sent back to his cell before the elements accommodated him? This bitter possibility gnawed at his thought and kept him awake.

Finally the winds piped up, and a wintry streak of bad weather set in.

At one o'clock in the morning Wilson slid out of bed, his alert eye on the sleeping figure of the keeper sitting by the hall doorway. He roused his comrade, took the sheets from both beds with him into the bath-room, quickly ripped them into long strips, knotted them together, and then let down his rope of escape, tying the upper end to the uncut bars of the window.

"Go first," he whispered to his confederate. "I'll be after you."

"You first," said the other man.

Wilson snapped the cut bars out of their places, laid them on the floor, squeezed his body through the narrow aperture, and let himself down his sheet rope, hand under hand.

The night was black as coal and shaken with wind and rain. The man sliding down that rope could not see a foot before him in the utter darkness, but this he counted an advantage. He must be nearly at the bottom now. His foot touched the earth. He threw out his chest, and sucked in the grateful cool.

"Well, Johnny," asked a voice at his shoulder, "out to take a little air?"

He felt the muzzle of a riot-gun pressed into his ribs, and heard the warder's high, mocking laugh. His confederate had betrayed him, in the hope of procuring a pardon for himself.

PART II. of this thrilling real-life narrative will be continued next week.

The Ghost of Gordon's Gap

OUR GREAT PINKERTON DETECTIVE SERIAL. This story is not fiction, but fact. It is the record of one of the most brilliant of the cases ever handled by Allan Pinkerton, America's real-life Sexton Blake.

THE FIRST CHAPTERS.

ALLAN PINKERTON is called in to investigate the mystery of a robbery and murder at Aggrington, a little Mississippi township.

The cashier of the bank, Alec McLeod, had been done to death. Pinkerton discovers that his murderer is the man who was his greatest friend, GEORGE SELLERS.

Pinkerton leaves the town, and later three of his detectives arrive to obtain the evidence necessary to convict Sellers by working on his superstition.

Whilst horseback-riding with JOHN ANDOVER, one of the detectives, Sellers sees the "ghost" of the murdered man. His nerves receive a further severe shock when he finds, scattered about his bedroom, quantities of blood.

These phenomena, the work of Pinkerton's three detectives, continue at intervals until Sellers is brought to the verge of panic, and the news of the strange apparitions are rumoured in the town.

(Now read on.)

A New Development.

IN the meantime, Pinkerton had returned to Chicago, feeling that he could safely leave the remainder of the scheme to the skill of his three operatives, with whom, however, he was to remain in constant touch by telegraph, and to whom he was to return at the hint of the now fast-approaching crisis.

Mrs. Mitchell still continued in her role of convalescent, and, whilst the injuries to her knee were mending, she slept in the next room to that of Sellers.

Some nights after the incident of the blood-trail she was lying awake in the small hours, in case anything should happen. It was well she was on the alert.

Suddenly, in the silence, she heard footsteps in the adjoining room, and, after listening for a space, heard Sellers descend the stairs, and pass out on to the veranda below.

Quickly putting on a dark cloak, she cautiously followed in his tracks, and saw him some distance off, making for the creek over almost the same path that she had sprinkled with the "blood."

On arriving by the stream, Sellers walked rapidly up and down indecisively, and then paused, looking straight before him as if in thought.

In the Creek.

Mrs. Mitchell crouched in the shelter of a bush, and then, greatly astonished, saw the man wade into the water. She started up, and was about to go after him, thinking he contemplated suicide, but she dropped back into hiding again as she saw him turn and begin walking up the bed of the shallow stream.

After a few yards he stopped, and put his hands under water, as if he were groping for something.

Then, apparently satisfied, he walked out of the water, and began to retrace his steps towards the house.

The watcher, seeing that he was on his way back, dodged on ahead of him unseen, and reached her bed-room only half a minute before a shuffling footfall in the next room announced that Sellers, too, had returned.

Next morning, as was to be expected, he made no mention whatever of his ramble in the small hours, and, indeed, said that he was feeling rather better than he had for some days. Nor were anybody's suspicious aroused, except those of Pinkerton's feminine operative, for Mrs. Sellers had been sleeping in her own room.

At the first opportunity Mrs. Mitchell communicated the facts to her colleague, Paul Dixon—or John Andover, as he was known in the town.

They discussed the affair from every angle, but neither of them could make out the man's object in exploring the bed of the stream, especially as he had in the daytime shown a marked aversion to the spot.

Pinkerton, too, was puzzled when the report of it reached him in Chicago. But he determined to make good use of the incident, should it be repeated. He replied, ordering that Stokes should lie in wait outside the house at nights, and if Sellers should emerge again, to shadow him, and, if possible, to give him another fright by appearing once again as the ghost of the murdered man.

Ignored!

This Stokes did, but he had a dreary time of it for the first four nights, as his vigil in the woods went unrewarded.

On the fifth, however, the expected happened.

As before, in the silence of the small hours a white figure emerged from the house. So silently did it move, and so eerie did it look in the moonlight, that the watcher was himself startled. Four nights had passed without incident, and, just as he was beginning to think he was wasting his time in being there at all, the man appeared, suddenly and weirdly.

However, Pinkerton's man soon pulled himself together, and, dressed as he was in the clothes that resembled those the murdered cashier used to wear, and ready to play the ghost at any moment, he followed Sellers as he passed his hiding-place.

The movements of the first occasion were now repeated almost exactly. Sellers proceeded to the creek, waded into the water and felt the gravel beneath. Then he emerged, and headed back to the house.

But here the procedure varied.

As Sellers reached a glade in the woods a ghostly figure passed before him, crossing from the shadows of the trees on one side to the shadows on the other. Sellers however, did not appear to notice him.

The manoeuvre was repeated, and this time Stokes made a distinct noise as he passed five yards in front of the other

But Sellers passed on without a sign the "ghost" had stood right in his path but was unheeded.

When the three detectives talked it over this puzzled them even more than the original incident had done, and Pinkerton was straightway informed of it.

Even he could not find any reason for Sellers having suddenly lost his fear for the apparition, especially when alone in the woods at night. But a thought flashed across his mind as an explanation for his delving in the bed of the stream.

Perhaps the money which had been stolen at the time of the murder might be concealed there! He remembered, too, that two gold pieces had been recovered by a negro near the spot just after the crime.

The Ghost Again!

When several days had gone by since Sellers had been confronted with the midnight spectre in the woods, and there seemed to be some grounds for believing he had altogether lost his dread of it, Andover was pleased to receive a suggestion from the man that they pass another few days on his plantation, which was some miles out of town.

Here, he knew, would be a good opportunity of deciding whether Sellers had conquered his fears or not, for it was at the plantation —or near it —that the 'ghost' had originally made such an impression on him.

This time the ladies signified their desire to visit the place, and, accordingly, in due course the party of four arrived at their destination.

There was a fifth member of it, however, who was not so much in evidence.

This was Stokes, who arrived by a roundabout way, and took up his station in a thick grove some distance from the plantation itself.

It was in this grove that Andover, on his second visit to the place, had been in hiding and watched Sellers measure off a number of paces, and examine the ground where he had stopped.

Andover had previously made all arrangements with the younger detective, and their plan was that, at a certain hour, he and Sellers would take a walk in that direction, when the ghost business was to be repeated and the results carefully watched.

Again Stokes was destined to a dreary vigil in the woods, which was only relieved by the stealthy, occasional visits of Mrs. Mitchell, or Andover, bearing food. It was not till the second night after the party's arrival that events so shaped themselves that the plot could be carried out.

The Ominous Grove.

It was just after supper, and in the gathering dusk, that Andover emerged from the homestead with Sellers, who had agreed to accompany him on a short walk before darkness set in. It so chanced that their steps led towards the grove in which the waiting Stokes was concealed.

Just after they had started, the two ladies, Mrs. Sellers and Mrs. Mitchell, also made up their minds to take a stroll, and set off after the menfolk, hoping to catch up to them.

Sellers was unusually cheery during the first part of the walk, but as he and Andover reached the edge of the grove he suddenly became depressed. When his companion suggested that they continue through it, he protested.

"No, don't go in that dreary place!" said Sellers. "Let's skirt the edge of it. I never like—"

He stopped, his face became white, and suddenly he let out a piercing scream.

Before them, passing with deliberate tread between the trees, was the ghost of Alec McLeod. Once again his face was death pallid, and the clotted crimson mass that marked the back of his head was thrown into greater relief by the pale features.

Sellers watched it like one condemned as it slowly passed out of sight behind some bushes, and then fell to the ground in a dead faint without so much as a groan.

Andover was bending over him and trying to revive him as the ladies came up. Fortunately, Mrs. Mitchell had some smelling-salts, and as the pungent fumes ascended his nostrils Sellers gradually came to.

The culminating episodes of this dramatic, real-life story will be recorded in the Supplement during forthcoming weeks.

Don't miss the end!

Policewomen in Rome?

By Zoe Beckley

The writer of this 'Policewomen' series went specially to Rome to discover the attitude of the Italian Police towards the employment of women in detective and police work. She found, however, that the Italian 'Politza' have no use for women in their profession, but she came away with many interesting details, which are recorded below.

[Photo: Daily Mirror.
This is a representative type of Italy's police, the Carabinieri. Note the stone "sentry-box" behind him.

I WAS sitting on a little plaza before Atrani's one handsome edifice, the cathedral. Its creamy facade rose against a sky so blue it seemed dyed. Below, some thirty feet, ran a ribbon of dusty road, bordered with an aged stone wall built, apparently, to keep the road from falling into the sea —a sparkling, cerulean sea.

As befits the visitor from a busy, northern land, I was contemplating the serenity of that Italian landscape, its freedom of life from such bustlings and rivalries as beset more up-to-date countries.

All was somnolent, heavy with the scent of orange blooms and fat lemons ripening in the sun.

Suddenly into the silence of my blue-and-golden dream, a queer sound crashed, as of a heavy object dropped. Then came a woman's voice in complaint.

I gazed over the parapet —everything was height over height, terrace upon terrace, wall above wall, and steps, forever steps and steps and steps —and I saw a peasant woman of the usual bare-foot type, broad-hipped and deep-chested, brown-skinned, and flashing-eyed.

She had flung down from its perch upon her head a great basket of lemons, and stood in the dusty road muttering and waving her work-worn hands.

It was as though her thoughts, held hard in check as she toiled in the gardens with the other workers, burst forth in the freedom of the open road, and had their way.

Enter the Police Patrol.

The little old man who presides over the cubby-box of the Customs, and takes the toll of "soldi" from each peasant who passes with wares to sell, looked curiously out, and fired a few staccato questions.

The woman made no answer, save to raise her voice to talk with new vigour. Two men mending nets on the steps of a mouldering stone house dropped their work and joined her, with the naive interest of all Latins in personal affairs.

The woman poured forth her grievances to all and sundry, gesticulating, lifting her eyes heavenward, appealing, demanding.

I could make nothing of it, and I'm not sure the men did, either.

Then, round a turn in the road, came the police patrol in his good, grey-green uniform, with his sword clanking, and his cape athwart a natty shoulder.

I had often seen the patrols and admired them. They act as policemen, traffic regulators, village counsellors, and supervisors in general of public behaviour.

Signor Patrol approached with dignity, and addressed the woman in soothing tones. It was exactly as though he had dropped a lighted match into a tank of petrol. Where smoke had issued, flames now leaped.

The woman railed and screamed, firing volleys of words, flashing darts from her big eyes, beating her breast with sturdy fists.

The little old customs collector, the net menders, and the military patrol were joined by a pair of teamsters, who stopped their straining mules and gaped with interest, proffering suggestions which only increased the woman's outcries.

The more the men argued, soothed, or shouted, the more hysterical she grew. The patrol lay a hand upon her arm. She flung it off fiercely. A postman came along and joined in the hullabaloo, which now reached the absolute extreme.

Hysterics.

Then from one of the obscure tunnels that form Atrani's streets emerged a woman, an infant on her hip.

She surveyed the pandemonium for an instant, and forthwith pushed capably through the knot of ineffectual males to where the victim of nerves, or what not, stood.

Followed a few quick words to the woman, a short speech to the men wholesale, and, to my astonishment, all became calm. The men moved off, muttering —the net menders to their job, the teamsters to the beating of their mules, the customs collector to the counting of his coppers, the postman to his route.

Only the patrol remained, fixing the hysterical one with a cold, official eye. Then he, too, moved on, and was lost to view behind a curve.

The woman with the baby jerked a thumb toward the basket of lemons the other had carried. Its owner picked it up, adjusted it upon her head, and strode away in sullen dignity.

And the woman with the babe gave a short, contemptuous laugh, just one note —"Ha!" like that— then retired to her tunnel.

To me, still hanging in riveted interest over my parapet, that laugh said:

"Stupid men! Gaping at a woman in a hysterical fit! Don't they know that the more they gape the more she'll carry on? She wants an audience. Remove the audience, and there's no more play."

At Police Headquarters.

I thought of this episode later, in Rome, when I went to ask the chief of police what part women play in detective crime in Italy.

There is a certain haphazardness and lack of modernity in the surroundings of this executive that might have given me a hint of current Italian methods.

The questura —police headquarters —occupies an ancient palace facing a courtyard behind a busy street.

You need to look where you are going. You hoist a foot unwarily, put it down where the step should be, and land with a jarring blup! You glare down to see why. A wedge-shaped piece is missing from the step's edge. It has been missing for a hundred and seventeen years. Nobody minds. The percentage of stumbles is fairly low.

Within are various long, shabby hallways, with rooms opening off for this and that civic purpose —licences, permissions, cards of identification, passports and vises.

Such desks and chairs as are present suffer more or less from decrepitude; walls are badly knocked and staircases creaky.

If you do not speak Italian, it may take you anything from twenty minutes to several hours to find the chief's quarters upstairs.

Somebody shows you a waiting-room, pathetically frowsy. A sofa is along one wall, a seatless chair near by, also several others with stuffing more or less hanging out.

One does not criticise. One knows that Italy is not rich, and that a populace that struggles for bread is scarcely concerned with the disrepair of a police office. All in good time.

A Puzzling Bequest.

I was at length ushered to the modest bureau of the first deputy and his interpreter, whose "Yes, missis," and "Now I tell to you, lady, best I can," in answer to my inquiries, held in them all the kindly courtesy in the world.

"Women deal efficiently with other women." I submitted, still remembering the episode on the Atrani road. "They know short cuts through one another's emotions to the underlying purposes. Do you set women to hunt women?"

The interpreter looked a little blank, but he translated me faithfully to Cavaliero Gaetano Laino, Commissario di Pelizia, Capo di Gabinetto di Roma, a small, swart man, very grave, very polite, and very much puzzled at me and my errand.

He considered seriously a moment. Then came the answer, carefully filtered through the cerebrations of the assistant:

"To understand what we do, or do not do, in the way of women crime detectors, we must look at our women criminals. Far back, hundreds of years, poisoning existed a fine art. Also, it was woman's speciality. You remember the Borgias?

"There were poison rings, with very small phials under the jewel, containing a deadly drop or two which, in a glass of wine, meant instant death; also poison pius, the smallest scratch from which was fatal. A touch, a handshake, and all was over.

The Psychology of the South.

"Deathdealing draughts were cunningly compounded, some leaving no discoverable trace, some that killed instantly, some that affected the victim as does a lingering illness.

"Those days are gone, and with them the crafty woman murderer. Life has become simple and full of hard labour. There is less time for intrigue. People's emotions have come more to the surface.

"Life is a matter of work, love, death. Crime grew simpler as life problems became mere elemental struggles. Premeditated crime has come to be rare —among women even rarer than with men.

"To-day the Italian woman is the last person capable of committing murder by poison."

Statistics on killings by poison, from 1835 to 1906, bear out the commissario. as follows: 1636-45, 465; 1846-55, 425; 1856-65, 356; 1866-75, 239; 1876-85, 142; 1886-95, 118; and 1896-1906, 18.

"The Italian woman," resumed Signor Laino, "is hot-tempered, quick, simple, devoted, and capable of hating passionately. She is a one-man woman. When the man is taken away —flash!

"The knife or revolver, whichever is handier. The knife is more deliberate, has to wait for opportunity, requires closer contact. But it is easier to reach. Any poor kitchen affords it. The pistol is a better weapon, but hard to get and costly.

"Most crimes that you call capital crimes are committed with the knife by peasants or villagers. In cities it is the revolver ninety times in the hundred.

Passion Let Loose.

"Italian women seldom commit other than capital crimes. A woman goes blind with anger or jealousy, shoots, and flings herself upon the mercy of the crowd. She plunges the knife, flees to her home, and sits sullenly brooding.

"She does not lay plans, or make careful escapes."

This was illustrated while I was in Rome.

Maria Abertanti, a girl of good family, followed her recreant sweetheart in the street as he was going to his office. When he refused to heed her she shot him four times with a revolver he had taken from an Austrian during the war, and given Maria as a souvenir. She made no attempt to escape, but backed against a wall and waited for the police to come to take her.

Commissioner Laino pointed out that capital crimes such as this increased greatly during the war. Since the war crime among women has sharply decreased, while crime by men has to even greater degree increased.

"Under modern conditions, and because the crimes of Italian women are simple and easy to detect," he said, "they present no great difficulties. We follow up and punish women just as we do men, using only male detectives."

Commissioner Laino, however, paid women the compliment of saying they should be extremely valuable as assistants to men in the detection of crime.

"In other countries," he added, with a deliberation that augurs ill for the Italian female with detective ambitions, "where women commit intellectual crimes —I mean crimes requiring thought, such as forgeries, swindling, and burglarising on a large scale— you are right in thinking a woman cannot deceive another woman as easily as she can a man.

Men Still Superior.

"In Italy a woman would not be so valuable for the reason that she still regards man as her superior. She is more in awe of a man than of another woman. She would give herself up to arrest by a man more quickly than to a woman."

But, upon arrest, a woman is searched by a woman instead of by a man. She is usually not a regular police attache, but a caretaker or cleaner or some petty employee about the building.

There are no regularly installed police matrons, but the women's sections of prisons are in charge of women supervisors and such.

It goes without saying that there are in Italy no policewomen like the stalwart "lady cops" of London or the efficient women police of New York. Young girls are not looked after in Rome or Naples as in many big cities of Europe and America. There is no women's court, no woman judge or counsellor. Not even in department stores do they have women detectives.

Women are, of course, in charge of institutions for the care of wayward girls. But many of these asylums are of a religious nature, under the care of Sisters, and connected in no way with processes of law.

From Commissioner Laino one gathers that woman presents no problem to the Italian police.

Too Dangerous for Woman.

Outside of petty thieving, it is said that eighty-five per cent of crimes committed in Italy by women are against either a man or a child. The fact that capital punishment does not exist in the country, and that due account is taken of the despair following love betrayal, has perhaps some tendency to simplify the problems of crime detection in regard to women. Crime is simple, detection easy, punishment not too drastic.

"I can only emphasise." said Commissioner Laino, "that we do not use women detectives because, our women criminals present no subtleties and complexities which would require special ferreting methods, and because, in such criminal categories as do require delicate, complex sleuthing, such as the cases of mafia and other secret organisations of blackmailers and murderers, our women are not of a type to engage in.

"These mafia societies are highly organised, and have a very intricate system of espionage upon the police themselves.

"It requires our bravest and most careful operatives to work in that field. Any police chief would hesitate to send a woman, however clever or brave, into work where the hazard of death is so high."

Opinions Differed.

One phase of sleuthing by women exists, which comes under no recognised head. It has nothing to do with the "black hand," and bears no relation to forms of violence rising from outraged love, desertion, neglect, and other accepted causes of feminine revenge.

It is an ultra-modern, purely local manifestation —the recent attempt to organise a society of women for secret service work.

These female amateurs were to parallel, after their own manner, the methods of the self-constituted male arbiters of thought and action composed chiefly of youth; their purpose is to break up by violent action any meetings expounding views contrary to their own.

Lately it happened in Rome that the principal of a children's school said in a speech that any women who joined such a movement were a disgrace to their sex. Women should stand, said he, for all that is love, peace, and the promotion of understanding.

One morning, while he was teaching at his school, a committee of these women called upon him.

They were formidable in type and in number, and insisted with appropriate firmness that he withdraw his remarks publicly.

The poor man, turning from his maps and blackboard, urged that the time and place were ill chosen to discuss the matter, as young children were looking on.

The women made a scene, caused a terrific uproar, and attacked the teacher with fists and nails. He fled through the yard, where two male members of the parallel organisation, hiding there, shot him dead in his tracks.

An account of the case appeared in the Roman newspapers in the early part of April, 1921

Nothing Doing!

Police Chief Laino has no apprehension on the score of this women's movement spreading.

"They did not." he points out. "even undertake this particular move from their own initiative. They were urged into it by their own men. In Italy men do the thinking. It is only Altabella who is the exception," he added, with a grin.

Altabella is the rather crabbed feminine leader of the organised women farmers and vineyard labourers who comprise some hundred thousand toilers in the vine terraces, and lemon, orange, and olive groves of South Italy.

When I had left the amiable Commissario di Polizia, Capo di Gabinetto, to stumble down the chipped and bitten stone steps into the cobbled courtyard, I felt a sudden strong sympathy with a woman I once heard speak in a small town.

It was at a club meeting, and the lady had been assigned as her subject, "Thibet." She arose with some nervousness.

"Ladies," said she, "I have been asked to talk to you about Thibet. I find, however, on looking it up, that there is practically nothing doing in Thibet."

I do not, however, despair of there being women detectives in Italy. Some day they will have running water quite commonly in hotel rooms. And motors in their fishing-boats. And typewriters instead of pen and ink. And steam heat instead of charcoal braziers. And a post-office system that requires less than forty minutes to get a letter registered. And traction power other than ox and mule and poor human muscle.

Italy is alive, industrially and politically speaking.

But when I have to speak on the subject of women police I have, alas! to report that there is practically nothing doing.

NEXT WEEK:

Policewomen in Paris.

CELLS-DE-LUXE.

SUPER-CELLS for the reception of West End guests have recently been opened at the new Marylebone police-station. Neither expense, effort, nor the ingenuity of the architect has been spared to fit the new cells up on what might reasonably be termed luxurious lines, and the prisoner who is lucky —or unlucky —enough to find himself incarcerated in them will have little to complain of beyond the temporary loss of his liberty.

No longer will the man who has dined well but not wisely be left to fall off his plank bed on to the hard, unsympathetic concrete floor. Instead he will be placed in a special cell provided with a movable cork floor or mat, which will not only prevent him from hurting himself, but which will prove quite as comfortable as the plank bed itself.

A careful survey has been made of all the reprehensible things a prisoner might want to do, and the cells have been planned to prevent him doing any one of them.

The walls are of a special glazed brick, on which it is almost impossible to write, thus preventing prisoners leaving messages for each other. Then, too, they can be more easily and efficiently cleaned.

The bell-push to summon the gaoler is so sunk into the wall that it would take a very clever man indeed to do any damage to it. The advantage of this, of course, is reaped by subsequent occupiers of the apartment.

The furniture is immovable, the radiators for heating are cunningly hidden, while the ventilators are in the roof out of reach. The windows, too, though serving their intended purpose quite efficiently, cannot be opened, and do not communicate directly with outer world. In fact, occupants of cells will be very clever indeed if they find opportunity for doing anything that is against the regulations.

Persons detained on suspicion are specially catered for, and will be accommodated in an apartment which only resembles a cell in that it is not possible to escape from it. Where innocence is established there will be no taint of prison association.

Imitative Crimes
By H. V. Tovey

It is the opinion of some criminologists that a large percentage of modern crime is due to the imitative faculty of weak-minded people. But whether this is so or not, it is a strange fact that from time to time the country is swept with a wave of crimes, each having very similar features, as the author of this informative article shows.

Miss Davidson, whose militant suffragette tactics were imitated by a madman.
[Photo: Daily Mirror.

IMITATION is said to be the sincerest form of flattery. Whether it is worth while, even from the criminal's point of view, is a matter for the criminal, male or female, to determine.

From the point of view of the police authorities imitative crime is punished with a severity equal to the original offence. Whether the perpetrators of imitative crimes are really criminals, or merely weaker minds, influenced by some sensational happening, is a matter best left to the scientific criminologist; enough for us to consider the fact that imitative crimes eddy round some tragic happening just as ripples ring round each other from a stone thrown into a pond.

117

Women Poisoners.

Notable crimes have always found imitators, even from the earliest days. In the early days of the world's history Roman women took to poisoning their husbands, and in the time of Henry VIII. poisoning by arsenic became so fashionable that poisoners were ordered by law to be boiled to death.

In Italy, in the seventeenth century, women sighed for freedom from the married state as they do to-day, and husband poisoning, owing to the imitative faculty of women, grew to such an extent that public steps were taken to punish women guilty of this crime.

Between 1872 and 1891 no fewer than sixty deaths from arsenical poisoning took place in Europe, England and America. This included the notorious Maybrick case, in which Mrs. Maybrick was said to have poisoned her husband by giving him arsenic extracted from fly-papers. Then the wave of imitation exhausted itself, and the imitative criminal had to wait for a new sensation.

A Gruesome Find.

In the year 1904 London was startled a grim "find."

A house in Ladysmith Road. Kensal Rise, had been let to a tenant, who, soon after he took possession, was startled at a most offensive odour, which caused him to complain to his landlord, who also lived in the other part of the house. This man, named Crossman, said he would have an old box removed which contained old clothes. He had this done, but so strong was the smell from the box that the carman engaged to do the job complained to the police, being under the impression that there was "something wrong."

How far he proved to be correct will be gathered that police inquiry showed that Crossman's wife disappeared in a most mysterious way. The box was opened, and the remains a woman were found cemented in it.

Crossman, becoming alarmed when he saw the police coming to his house, ran away across some fields, and when about to be caught, stopped and cut his throat with a razor, dying before help could be obtained.

Arthur Devereux.

In the following year Arthur Devereux, a chemist, was arrested for what was known as the "Trunk Mystery." He had killed his wife and two children, and buried their remains in a large trunk, which he had left at a warehouse, "to be called for."

Devereux, his wife, and children had mysteriously disappeared, and the wife's mother, becoming alarmed at the absence of news from her daughter, went to the house, to find that all the furniture had been removed to a warehouse in Buller Road, Kensal Rise.

On inquiry there she found that all that remained was a trunk, strongly strapped, sealed, and corded.

The police were called in, and their suspicious were aroused by the fact that the keyhole of the trunk was even stopped with wax. The trunk was opened, and the bodies of the woman and her two children were found huddled into it, covered with layers of cement and glue.

Both these tragedies took place within a quarter of a mile of each other. They also resembled each other in the fact that both men were proved to have been bigamists, Crossman having had eight wives, and Devereux three or four.

Nine Unsolved Mysteries.

Another coincidence was that the trunks in each case were put in the same room in the mortuary after they had come into the hands of the police.

Attacks on women during recent years seem to have followed similar lines, and generally with the same object.

That of the most recent date is the Bournemouth crime, in which Miss Wilkins was lured to her death by the man Allaway who recently paid the death penalty for his crime. In all these cases the woman was lured to some isolated spot, or trapped in some way so as to render assistance impossible.

Since May, 1919, there have been nine such cases, all suggesting the imitative faculty of the weak, ill balanced criminal mind.

In none of these cases have the police been able to trace the perpetrator of the crime.

Crimes in Woods.

Expert criminologists attribute this outbreak to the blood-lust engendered during the war; but, be that as it may, each of these exhibited the same cold blooded disregard of life, and in no case could there be traced any reason for the murder, beyond, the imitative criminal instinct.

There was the case of the pretty young W.A.A.C., Miss Nellie Rault, who, after being missing for some time, was found stabbed to death near Haynes Park Camp, Bedford.

Within a few months of this tragedy was that of Louisa Gates.

She was missing from home, and found dead in Hangman's Wood. The method of her death is still a mystery, for her body had lain so long that no expert could determine to what cause it was due. There was no question but that it was foul play, for there was no reason why she should have taken her own life.

Another startling mystery was the death of Mrs. Buxton, licensee of the Cross Keys, a Chelsea public-house. She was found dead at the foot of the stairs leading to the cellars by firemen, who went to the house to extinguish a fire which had broken out in some unknown fashion.

Circumstances suggested that an attempt had been made to set fire to the body, so as to hide all traces of the crime.

Purposeless Murders.

Then came the case of Mrs. Ridgley, the Hitchin shopkeeper, who was found dead in her shop nearly a day after her death, killed by some person, presumably a man, for no known reason.

Nothing was taken worth having, so that robbery was not the motive. Here again comes the suggestion of some imitative crime —a sudden blood lust on the part of some unbalanced brain affected by recent crimes of a similar character.

Similar in character to this was the case of the Cambridge shopkeeper, Miss Lawn, who was found dead in her shop, killed by some unknown hand, cruelly battered to death. Again robbery was not the motive, and a fairly large sum of money was found in the house, while the minor sum taken from the shop till may have been but a "red herring across the trail," just to lead the police on a wrong scent. Though a man was tried for this murder, he was acquitted.

Another purposeless murder was that of Miss Bella Wright, who was lured on to an open but secluded road near Leicester, and there shot dead.

Like the foregoing, and equally tragic, was the death of Catherine Daley, who was found stabbed to death in her room in Walworth. There was no suggestion of a motive for this crime, except the imitative faculty which seemed to flood the country at the time.

By no means the least of these was the murder of Miss Shore, the pretty nurse, who was found brutally murdered in a Hastings train. Neither motive nor clue was ever found to account for this frenzy of murder against a harmless, inoffensive woman.

A Derby Tragedy.

Two striking cases of auto-suggestion occurred in 1913, both, strangely enough, connected with racing. Both these, without doubt, were due to imitation.

At the Epsom Summer Meeting of 1913, during the race for the Derby, Miss Davidson, a militant suffragette, ran on to the course and interfered with the King's horse. She was knocked down and killed.

One of her colleagues, Harold Hewitt, an equally ardent advocate of women's suffrage, attempted the same tactics at Ascot. During the running for the Ascot Gold Cup he ran on to the course waving a white, green, and purple flag in one hand, and waving a loaded revolver in the other, just as the horses came abreast of him.

He called to Whalley, the jockey of Tracery, as the mare was opposite the Holloway Gate, "Hold up!"

Whalley took no notice, however, and Hewitt threw both arms round the mare's neck, bringing horse and rider on top of him.

Whalley was rendered unconscious, and so was Hewitt, who received a fractured skull for his share in the scene. Hewitt was sent to a lunatic asylum, from which he escaped, going to British Columbia. Some years later he surrendered himself, and, after trial, was sentenced to two days' imprisonment, the judge holding that he was not in his right mind at the time, and further, that he had been influenced by the act of Miss Davidson.

Here, again, we have the imitative faculty in crime strongly defined.

Recent Cases.

Two other cases which appeared to run on parallel lines were those in which Greenwood and the man Armstrong were concerned. Greenwood was, however, acquitted, so though the facts of the cases seemed identical to a certain point, the likeness was not complete to the full extent.

Beyond doubt, the imitative faculty is responsible for the recent "dope" craze. Women and men, possessed with the idea that it is "the thing" to do, because they see others doing the same thing, have allowed themselves to become drug fiends, rendering themselves irresponsible for their actions, and the prey to impressions from outside sources.

There was the case of Ronald True, the suicide of Freda Kempton, the strange death of Billie Carlton, and others, all due to "dope," and all due to the fact that the actors' minds in these dramas became obsessed by what had happened in the other cases.

Modern Raffles.

The old-time burglar and country house thief has been superseded by the modern "Raffles," whose scores of imitators arose through the fact that detection was difficult, owing to their position in Society, and the imitative impulse that prompted them to do as others had done, with profit to themselves and the glamour of imitation.

Perhaps the most remarkable and the most recent of imitative crimes has been the series of raids on post-offices, in which armed youths have "held up" officials employed in the various local post-offices, and have stolen wads of notes intended for the payment of pensions intended for disabled soldiers and others.

Since the first of these there has been a succession of some twenty or more, in which the perpetrators have escaped owing to of lack of identification.

Showing the Way.

Public interest in crime, an interest that will never be suppressed as long as human nature is what it is, may be responsible for this imitative faculty. It may be, too, that the familiarity with death in its most gruesome forms, and the frequent handling of weapons of destruction, may have their share in prompting criminals to take the most familiar, the most easy way, out of a difficulty, especially when someone has shown them just "how to do it."

Crime waves, like waves of gambling, waves of extreme fashion, and other abnormal outbreaks, have their periods, and criminologists believe, and with reason, that the sequence of imitative crimes will exhaust itself, as other waves have done, when once the stress due to the nerve strain of the war has run its course.

Criminals have always to bear in mind the one unalterable fact that, imitative crime generally meets the same punishment as the original offence.